PUFFIN BOOKS

Loving *Spirit*
Hopes

Linda Chapman lives in Leicestershire with her husband, three children, two dogs and a pony. When she is not writing, she spends her time looking after her family, reading, talking to people about writing, and horse riding whenever she can.

You can find out more about Linda on her websites: *lindachapman.co.uk* and *lindachapmanauthor.co.uk*

LINDA CHAPMAN

Loving Spirit

Hopes

PUFFIN

PUFFIN BOOKS

Published by the Penguin Group
Penguin Books Ltd, 80 Strand, London WC2R ORL, England
Penguin Group (USA) Inc., 375 Hudson Street, New York, New York 10014, USA
Penguin Group (Canada), 90 Eglinton Avenue East, Suite 700, Toronto, Ontario, Canada M4P 2Y3
(a division of Pearson Penguin Canada Inc.)
Penguin Ireland, 25 St Stephen's Green, Dublin 2, Ireland (a division of Penguin Books Ltd)
Penguin Group (Australia), 250 Camberwell Road, Camberwell, Victoria 3124, Australia
(a division of Pearson Australia Group Pty Ltd)
Penguin Books India Pvt Ltd, 11 Community Centre, Panchsheel Park, New Delhi – 110 017, India
Penguin Group (NZ), 67 Apollo Drive, Rosedale, Auckland 0632, New Zealand
(a division of Pearson New Zealand Ltd)
Penguin Books (South Africa) (Pty) Ltd, 24 Sturdee Avenue, Rosebank, Johannesburg 2196, South Africa

Penguin Books Ltd, Registered Offices: 80 Strand, London WC2R ORL, England

puffinbooks.com

First published 2011
001 – 10 9 8 7 6 5 4 3 2 1

Text copyright © Linda Chapman, 2011
All rights reserved

The moral right of the author has been asserted

Set in Sabon 12/16pt
Typeset by Palimpsest Book Production Limited, Falkirk, Stirlingshire
Printed in Great Britain by Clays Ltd, St Ives plc

British Library Cataloguing in Publication Data
A CIP catalogue record for this book is available from the British Library

ISBN: 978-0-141-32834-8

www.greenpenguin.co.uk

Penguin Books is committed to a sustainable
future for our business, our readers and our
planet. This book is made from paper certified
by the Forest Stewardship Council.

*To all my friends who have shared
the madness . . .*

Do not stand at my grave and weep;
I am not there.
I do not sleep.

From 'Do Not Stand at My Grave and Weep'
by Mary Frye (1932)

Listen and I will speak
Ask and I will answer

Spirit . . .

The grey horse stood in the field, his dark eyes wise, his tail swishing softly to keep away the flies. Near the gate, the other horses jostled, teeth flashing and hooves threatening as they argued over patches of grass and the water trough. The grey horse never got involved in their disputes. He led a small group of quieter horses. When he moved, so did they.

Lifting his head, he snorted with contentment. The early summer grass was lush and green, and the sun was warming his back. Behind the field the mountains of the Peak District rose up, their slopes criss-crossed with grey stone walls and dotted with black-faced sheep. The horse coughed, feeling a tightening sensation deep inside his chest. He paused in his grazing, but then, accepting the discomfort, he lowered his head and started cropping the grass again. He had known far worse pain in his life.

The memories were always there. The man who had fallen off him, coming to his stable, whip in hand. The horse could remember the feel of the whip lashing down on his neck and shoulder, and the man's anger that he hadn't understood. The scars had left him unfit for the show ring and so he had gone to another home – a trekking stable where they had made him carry people up the mountains hour after hour, his tack stiff, his stomach empty, his coat thick with mud and grease. The horse remembered his life there too – the tiredness, the hunger, the shouting when he slowed.

It was over now. He looked to the gate, his eyes seeking the slim blonde girl with her soft hands and gentle voice. The girl who had saved him. The horse coughed, feeling the strain in his chest again. Putting his head down, he continued to graze, his eyes never leaving the gate. She wasn't there yet but he knew she would come . . .

Chapter One

The stable was warm, the air close and still. Outside on the busy yard there were sounds of stable doors banging, hooves clattering on concrete, grooms calling to each other. Ellie pushed the body brush over Spirit's grey coat, cleaning it with every stroke of the curry comb. Her mind emptied as she lost herself in the regular rhythm – *brush and clean, brush and clean . . .*

Back in February, when she had bought Spirit at a horse sale, he'd been thin and scarred, destined to go for meat, but as soon as Ellie saw him, she had felt a connection between them. From the moment she'd looked into his eyes, she'd known she couldn't leave the sale without him and so she had bought him and walked him back through the bitterly cold wind to High Peak Stables where she lived. He looked like a different horse nowadays: his white mane and tail tangle-free, his once-dirty coat clean. Ellie ran a hand over his side, pleased with the velvet-soft feel. However, she could feel his ribs bumping too sharply against her fingers. Although Spirit had put on weight after she'd brought him back from the sale, over the last couple of weeks he had gone off his food and was growing thinner again. She frowned, worried, as she looked at his tucked-up stomach. Why wasn't he eating?

'Should we talk?' she whispered, putting down the grooming tools. When she and Spirit were quiet and still, her mind could connect with his. Sometimes they would communicate with words; sometimes he would send her images and feelings that she would interpret.

At first, Spirit had been the only horse Ellie had been able to communicate with, but then he had shown her how to talk to other horses too. Now, if horses were unhappy or in pain and people didn't know why, Ellie could find out. No one knew about her ability, only Spirit.

Shutting her eyes, she placed a hand on his shoulder and began to breathe deeply and slowly, clearing her mind, sending out love. Every person and animal in the world had their own energy field. Being able to talk to an animal with her thoughts involved opening herself up and connecting to that energy, waiting for the images and words to come. Every bit of her mind was focused on Spirit. Gradually she felt the familiar sensation as their minds merged. It was as if a door was opening.

Spirit?

Yes.

A thrill ran through Ellie. Even though she had talked to Spirit many times like this it always felt amazing when he answered.

How are you feeling today? Opening her eyes, she moved closer to him. Spirit had arthritis and his joints were often stiff. Maybe they were hurting now and she wondered if that was why he hadn't been eating. *Is your arthritis all right?*

Yes.

Are you sure? You haven't been eating your food.

I don't feel hungry.

But you're losing weight.

Spirit sent her a wave of reassurance in reply. A picture of him as a foal came into her mind. He was cantering around a field. It was one of his early memories and Ellie experienced it now as if she was him. She could feel the sun on her back, the cool grass under her feet. She felt the instinctive urge to gallop and buck in delight. Happiness surged through her and she knew she was feeling what Spirit had felt back then.

She wondered why he was showing her the memory – what he was trying to say. *You were happy then?* she questioned.

Yes. It is how I feel now.

Ellie breathed a sigh of relief. If Spirit didn't think

there was anything wrong that was good enough for her. She rested her head against his neck and changed the subject.

I managed to speak to Gem this morning, Spirit. I wanted to find out why he's always so tense.

Gem was one of the hunter ponies she rode for her uncle. He was only young, a blue roan pony, and about to start his first season of showing. Ellie loved him like she loved all the ponies on the yard, but she found him quite difficult to ride because he was so anxious and needed constant reassurance. She'd been keen to find out more about him and his past.

What did he tell you?

Ellie began to share Gem's thoughts with Spirit, showing him the pictures the pony had shared with her earlier that day – the first memories from when Gem had been with his mother in the field and then the day he had been taken away from her. Ellie had lived through the moments with him – as he had walked inquisitively up to the man with the headcollar and then been put into a horsebox with three other foals. There had been noise and confusion, men shouting, the other foals whinnying frantically.

Ellie had felt Gem's terror as the ramp had clanged shut. He'd been very young to be separated from his mother – only four months old. There had been the smell of diesel fumes from the engine and the fear radiating from the other foals. She had heard his desperate cries for his mother as the horsebox started moving away. He'd never seen his mother again.

Gem had told her he'd been taken to a showing yard where he stayed for a couple of years. There he had been fed and watered, but the grooms were busy. After his attempts at seeking affection – nuzzling, pushing against them, pulling at their clothes – had been met with slaps and sharp words, he became nervous. When he was old enough to be ridden he'd been sold on again, this time coming to High Peak Stables, Ellie's uncle's yard in north Derbyshire.

Scared and bewildered, Gem had arrived in the autumn, just eight months ago. He had been broken in and taught to wear a saddle and bridle. Too scared to fight, he had accepted a rider without protest. But Ellie had felt an anxiety deep within him about what would happen next in his life.

It's OK, she'd told him, longing to take his nervousness away. *Nothing bad's going to happen. You're safe here.* Her uncle was firm and hard with his horses, but he wasn't cruel to them. *And I'm here to look after you now. I'll love you, ride you, groom you.*

The young pony had sighed and rested his head against her chest as she talked to him. She'd felt his relief wash over her that finally someone was listening.

I think I can make him happier, Ellie told Spirit.

Now that he trusts me and I know why he's nervous. I'll try to help more.

She felt Spirit's warm breath on her hands and felt his pleasure. *Good.*

Ellie put her arms round his neck. *Thank you*, she told him. *Thank you for showing me how to talk to other horses. I want to help as many as I can.*

Spirit snorted softly and Ellie felt love well up inside her. The bond between them was so strong. She couldn't imagine how her life would be now if she hadn't bought him that day at the sale.

Rubbing his forehead, she reluctantly stepped back, letting their thoughts separate again. She could stay talking to him for hours, but there was too much to do on the yard.

'I'd better go.' She gave him a last hug. 'I'll see you later.'

Picking up the grooming kit, Ellie left the stable, her heart light. She stopped to greet the black gelding in the next stable along. He was a valuable show hack called Lucifer. When he had first arrived back in March, he'd been very unhappy on the yard, but eventually Ellie had talked to him and worked out why. After that, she'd been able to help him settle in.

I wonder which horse I'll talk to next, Ellie thought as she headed towards the main yard. She'd love to talk to all the horses there, but it was hard to find the time. It wasn't something that could be rushed.

Some horses would talk straight away but with others she would often have to just stand for a long while, waiting until they relaxed and their minds connected with hers. She would happily have given up the hours needed, but now it was May there were shows nearly every Saturday and Sunday, often in the week too, and her uncle had a constant list of jobs for her to do. It was hard enough finding the time just to groom and ride Spirit.

Ellie reached the main yard. Here a large courtyard was enclosed by ten spacious loose boxes. The remaining twenty horses were stabled in two American-style barns. The countryside around the stables was majestic and wild. Somehow the peaks of the north Derbyshire mountains that rose up behind the yard looked bleak and untamed even in the middle of summer with the sun shining. In contrast, the yard was an enclave of order and control. Headcollars were hung neatly from hooks and the yard was perfectly swept. High Peak Stables was one of the top showing yards in the country and her uncle, its owner, Len Carrington, believed in neatness and order at all times.

As Ellie reached the yard, she saw her sixteen-year-old cousin, Joe, leading a chestnut pony with a flaxen mane and tail out of the pony barn. Stuart, the yard manager, was lunging a horse in the small schooling ring by the car park, while Helen and Sasha, the two grooms, were cleaning tack in the sun. Luke – Joe's cousin from the other side of the family, who also worked full-time for Len – was going out on a hack on one of the hunters. Everyone on the yard was always busy. Len had huge amounts of energy himself and would not tolerate any slacking. Anyone found not working could expect a torrent of sharp words. The days started at 7 a.m. or earlier and often didn't finish until late at night if there was a show on.

It was a completely different life from the one Ellie used to have. She had grown up in New Zealand with her dad, Len's younger brother, who had been a vet, and her mum who had been a kindergarten teacher. Ellie had been very happy. She and her mum kept horses and ponies, and she used to travel with her dad on his vet rounds. But ten months ago her world had turned upside down when both her parents were killed in a car accident. At first Ellie had lived with her gran, but her gran was old and in January it was decided that Ellie should move to England to live with Len and Joe. She would never forget her arrival – how she had hated her uncle, hated the oppressive grey skies of the Peak District, hated being torn away from her home. But after she and Joe became friends and she found Spirit, her life had started to improve.

Her mum used to have a saying: *every ending is a new beginning*. Recently Ellie had begun to think how true that was. Her old life had ended, but this new one had started. If she hadn't moved from New Zealand, she would never have met Spirit or discovered she could talk to horses. She would always, always wish her parents were still alive, but she did find comfort in the truth of the saying, and slowly but surely High Peak Stables was beginning to feel more like home.

Joe had helped with that, Ellie thought, smiling at her cousin taking Milly to the wash-barn. Joe had been welcoming from the moment she arrived and now they were the closest of friends. For a while it had seemed they might become more than that, but although Ellie hadn't seen them being cousins as a problem, Joe had, so eventually they'd decided to remain just as friends.

Ellie went over, feeling slightly guilty for having spent so long with Spirit. 'Do you want some help with Milly?'

The chestnut pony was pawing the concrete on the yard. She was completely different from Gem, a feisty outgoing ball of energy who fidgeted constantly. It was one of the things Ellie loved about horses; they all had their own personalities, just like people and they all needed different handling.

'If you've got time,' Joe replied, pushing his sandy brown hair from his forehead, where it kept falling. 'I've read about a new way to persuade her to stand still in one of my books,' he went on. 'Can you fetch the hosepipe for me?'

'Sure.' Ellie put the grooming kit down and pulled out the hosepipe. 'So, what are you going to do?'

Joe loved exploring new ways of training horses. He read a lot of books by trainers who were into natural horsemanship, people who believed in working with horses in a partnership rather than using force.

'Well, rather than shouting at her and trying to *make* her stand still like we usually do while I bathe her, I'll let her move – but make her move more than she wants to, so in the end it'll hopefully persuade her that standing still is better. You'll see what I mean when I do it. Come closer with the hose, just one step at a time. We'll only do her tail and legs, the rest of her is clean.'

Ellie started walking towards Milly with the hose. Milly stood still and he praised her, but then as Ellie came closer the chestnut pony started to swing round. Rather than stopping her, Joe let her move, but began turning her in a tight circle. At first Milly moved round swiftly because it was what she had wanted to do, but when Joe continued to make her turn she began slowing down, only he wouldn't let her stop for ten whole circles. When he did halt her, she was so glad to be still that she stood quietly while he praised her by rubbing between her eyes.

'OK, come closer again,' he told Ellie.

Ellie took another step closer with the hosepipe. Immediately the pony started to move again. Joe patiently repeated exactly what he had done before, turning her round and round, stopping after ten circles to praise her.

'Try again,' he told Ellie.

This time, Ellie saw Milly hesitate before moving. It was as though she realized that if she tried to move she would have to move far more than she wanted to. She stood still until Ellie was right beside her tail this time, then she fidgeted. Joe repeated the turning all over again. This time, when he stopped, Ellie saw the understanding in the pony's eyes. By staying calm and patient and repeating things, Joe was making it very clear to her what he wanted – if she stood still she was praised; if she moved she had to turn in a lot of circles.

'Shall I try again?' Ellie asked.

Joe nodded, stroking Milly and murmuring softly to her now that she was still. This time Milly stood as Ellie began to hose her tail and legs and rub in shampoo. She was a quick learner and although they had to break off a couple more times to repeat the process, by the time they had finished washing her, Milly had learnt the lesson and was standing perfectly. Joe was able to put the leadrope over her neck and not even tie her up.

'That's made such a difference!' Ellie said in delight. 'And it's so simple!'

'I know.' Joe looked pleased. 'It's all from this book I've been reading about making the right thing easy and the wrong thing hard work, then letting the horse choose which it wants to do, rather than getting into a fight and shouting at her to stand still.'

They smiled at each other over Milly's neck. Ellie wished she could tell Joe how she talked to horses – she had tried once, but even he had found it too hard to believe.

It was hard for Ellie to keep such a big thing a complete secret though, particularly when she could help so many different horses on the yard. Her uncle and Stuart put her ideas down merely to natural horse sense and good instincts. But she longed for someone to know it was more than that.

She wondered if the alternative techniques Joe had started using recently would make him more open to what she could do.

'Joe.' Ellie ducked under Milly's neck.

'What?'

Ellie took his hands. This was going to be hard. 'If I tell you something weird, will you promise to try and believe me?'

'I guess,' Joe said curiously. 'What is it?'

But before she could say any more, there was the sound of hooves and Len appeared, leading Solomon, a steel-grey novice hunter, down from the main schooling ring. Ellie quickly dropped Joe's hands.

'What's happening here?' Her uncle's blue-grey eyes were the same colour as Ellie's but his were granite-like. His weather-beaten face furrowed as he looked at them.

'Nothing.' Ellie felt flustered as she realized he'd seen her holding Joe's hands.

'Ellie was just about to tell me something,' Joe said.

'Nothing important,' Ellie added hastily.

Her uncle looked sharply between them, but to Ellie's relief he was distracted by Milly. 'What's that mare doing not tied up?' he demanded.

'She doesn't need to be,' Joe replied.

'Doesn't need to be?' Len stared as if he'd gone mad. 'She'll be off like a bleedin' rocket any moment. Don't be daft, Joe. Tie her up.'

'She's fine, Dad. I've been teaching her to stand still. I read about it in my books. You give them a choice and –'

'Choice! She's a horse, not a flamin' person!' Len snapped. He seemed to be in one of his darker moods that day. 'You and your ruddy books!'

'But this way really works, Dad. It –'

'Oh for –' Len broke off and swore. 'Just get that bloody pony tied up, Joe! I'm not risking her running off and breaking her leg just because you fancy yourself as some kind of horse whisperer. And you stand up there!' he growled to Solomon who was moving round. The horse continued to fidget. '*Stand!*' Len hit the horse in the stomach with his hand. The horse threw his head in surprise, but then stood still.

Ellie saw Joe's shoulders tighten, but she knew he wouldn't object or argue with Len. Without saying another word, he tied Milly up.

Ellie found it harder not to say anything. She bit her lip as she wished she could speak *for* Joe, telling her uncle how ignorant he was being. But Ellie had her own reasons for holding back – she needed to be able to keep Spirit on the yard. High Peak Stables was so isolated there were no other yards nearby where she could move Spirit to. If she angered Len, especially when he was in one of his really black fault-finding moods, there was a real danger that he would refuse to let her keep Spirit there.

'Where's Luke?' Len demanded. 'I need a hand shifting some feed sacks.'

'He's out on a ride,' Joe answered. 'I . . . I could help.'

'You?' Len snorted derisively. 'You're as much use as a wet paper bag when it comes to things like that! I need Luke.'

Ellie glared. Her uncle was so unfair. Joe worked incredibly hard, but he couldn't help being slimly

buil
She
beer
him
sens
insid
to ha
had i
a sho
a cha
wait
to list
away.
    Len
he ord

she started to untack him. There wa

thing more to do on the yard.

That night, when everythi
the show the next da
washed, the tack cle
went to Spirit's s

Len, Joe and
was quiet
trottin

As

Ellie let out a muttered exclamation as soon as he was out of earshot. 'He drives me mad!' She looked at Solomon. 'He didn't even say please.'

'What did you expect? You know Dad,' Joe said. '*Do this. Do that.* You just have to do it.'

'Or get yelled at.'

'Or worse.' Joe frowned. 'I don't know why he's in such a mood today. He seemed OK when he took Solomon up to the school. Oh, well.' He changed the subject. 'We'd best get on. I'll put Milly away and sort the horsebox ready for the show tomorrow. Can you untack Solomon and then wash Fizz?'

'Sure,' Ellie said. Patting the grey hunter's neck,

ng was finally ready for
, the ponies groomed and
ned, the horsebox packed, Ellie
able. The grooms had left now and
Luke were all in the house. The yard
and peaceful, with only the occasional cat
by. Spirit was lying down on his straw bed.
he let herself in, he whickered softly, his eyes
ghting up.

'Hey, boy.' Ellie crouched down next to him and he nuzzled her hands. She let out a deep sigh. Nothing beat the feeling of being with Spirit. Settling down beside him, she put her arm over his back, feeling tiredness wash over her. She wondered whether to talk to him, but she didn't have the energy left. It was enough just to sit with him in the peace and quiet. Even though their minds weren't connected, she could feel the love and comfort coming from him.

'Oh, Spirit, I'm so lucky to have you,' Ellie murmured.

She stroked his side, feeling the bump of his ribs under her fingers. But at least he had eaten more of his feed that night. She'd made a bran mash and added extra carrots and molasses to it, stroking him and hand-feeding him. He'd finished almost the whole bucket with her beside him.

Maybe he'd just been bored with his old feed? But then he would have told her that, surely? Ellie felt a flicker of worry creeping up inside her, but forced her anxiety down. He'd eaten tonight's feed – that was the main thing.

'I'll feed you up again,' she promised him. 'Even if I have to hand-feed you every day. You'll soon put on weight.'

She rested her head against his neck. She hadn't thought it was possible to love anyone or anything as much as she loved Spirit. She'd have to go in into the house for supper soon, but for now it was just her and Spirit wrapped in a circle of warmth and contentment and it was the only place in the world she wanted to be.

Chapter Two

It was a very early start the next day to travel to the show down south. The ponies were loaded into the horsebox at 3 a.m. and then Len set off on the long drive. Ellie and Helen travelled inside the horsebox, while Luke went with Len in the cab. None of the ponies Joe rode were competing that day, so he stayed on the yard with Stuart and Sasha. Ellie knew he'd be glad not to be there. He'd ridden in shows all his life but was much happier at home, working with the horses. Ellie found it hard to imagine feeling like that. She loved everything about showing, from preparing the ponies to actually riding in the ring, and whenever she was placed or won she felt amazing. It was the biggest buzz ever!

As the horsebox chugged along the winding roads of the Peak District, heading for the motorway, Ellie and Helen settled down to rest. The living accommodation of the horsebox was like an incredibly luxurious caravan, with a leather sofa and smart small kitchen, wide-screen TV and two sleeping spaces, one above the cab and one above the horses. There was a shower and toilet, and every available space inside had cupboards built into it for storage.

Helen went to sleep in the bed above the horses, while Ellie put her iPod on and curled up on the sofa with a blanket. She was glad Helen was the groom that day. Helen was in her late twenties and, although she was quiet, she was friendly. Sasha, the pretty, blonde junior groom, on the other hand, always ignored Ellie. She went out with Luke and spent all her free time with him or just talking to Helen. Ellie had the strong impression Sasha didn't like her and now, as she chose a different track on her iPod, she wondered if it had anything to do with the fact that over the last few months she and Luke had become better friends.

An image of Luke came into her head as she pulled the blanket around her. Tall and dark-haired, with glinting blue eyes, he was undeniably attractive and always had a string of girls ringing him and wanting to go out with him. At first, Ellie had really disliked him. He'd seemed so flippant and arrogant, not caring about anything or anyone, but over the last few months she'd realized there was another, more complex, side to him.

Luke hadn't had the easiest of childhoods. Although his parents were rich, they spent little time with him, sending him to various expensive boarding schools, and he'd spent most of his holidays with Len and Joe. He'd once told Ellie that Len had been more of a father to him than his own dad had ever been. Knowing that her uncle – so often cold, hard and bullying – was the best dad Luke had ever known made Ellie feel sorry for him. And beneath the don't-care front she knew that he did care about some things. He was incredibly focused when it came to shows and he was very open-minded, prepared to try anything if it would help a horse perform better. She'd been working with him on Lucifer, who he often rode, and together they'd made a massive difference to how Lucifer behaved.

She just wished he would let his nice side show through more. When he was flippant, he drove her mad. For a moment, she remembered how a few weeks ago he'd laughingly asked her if she ever wondered what it would be like if the two of them got together. And yet he was still going out with Sasha! As if she ever would anyway – Luke had to be the most unfaithful person of all time. Sasha was welcome to him.

Ellie pushed Luke to the back of her mind and quickly turned her thoughts to the show. Milly had been really naughty in the ring the week before, fidgeting and spinning round whenever she was supposed to stand still. Ellie had been told off by her uncle and had since been working hard with Milly – she hoped the practice was going to pay off.

Sighing, she pulled the blanket closer. She was getting sleepy. Shutting her eyes, she lost herself in her music and drifted off.

They arrived at the show ring at 6 a.m. Len had four horses at the show that day – Milly, who was in the 14 hands-high show hunter pony class; Zak, who Luke was riding in the intermediate show hunter class; and Fizz and Bill, owned by a client called Veronica Armstrong. Her children came for lessons with Len and he prepared their ponies for the show ring. Ellie couldn't imagine having a pony and not looking after it, only seeing it at a show or when having lessons. Privately she thought the Armstrongs were very annoying: Emmie had just turned five and was always whingeing, and Oliver was ten and just wanted to play on his portable PlayStation, while their mother was constantly fussing around them. But they were Len's clients and Ellie knew she had to be polite and helpful. She helped Helen prepare Fizz and then escaped to work Milly in, just as she heard Emmie Armstrong's shrill voice coming towards the horsebox. 'But why can't I have an ice cream? I *want* one!'

Ellie thankfully rode Milly away to the outskirts of the show ground. The sky was cornflower-blue, and white cow parsley billowed at the sides of the field like drifts of snow. Milly pulled excitedly at the reins, every muscle in her body tense with excitement, her nostrils flaring.

'Steady, girl,' Ellie murmured soothingly. Happiness welled up deep inside her – she loved this time at a show ground, when everything was just starting and the whole day stretched ahead, full of possibilities.

She moved Milly into a trot, circling her and riding through the different paces, asking her to back up and stand. When she was happy that Milly had settled down and was listening to her, she rode her back to the horsebox to start preparing her for the ring. The Armstrongs had left to take part in the lead-rein class with Fizz.

Ellie plaited Milly's mane in the peace and quiet, then groomed her thoroughly. It was hot work and Ellie stripped down to her jodhpurs and blue vest top. She had almost finished and was running a cloth over Milly's shining conker-brown coat, when Luke rode up on Zak.

'Looking good!' Luke said. He was in his work clothes, grey jodhpurs and T-shirt, showing off his tanned, muscular arms. He dismounted effortlessly, throwing a leg over the front of the saddle.

'Thanks,' Ellie said, pleased.

Luke grinned. 'Milly looks all right too.'

Ellie blushed and turned away, hearing Luke chuckle. She knew he was just teasing her and she cursed herself for reacting. The last thing he needed was someone boosting his ego even more!

'So, are you looking forward to your class?' Luke asked as he started removing Zak's tack.

Glad to be on safer ground, talking about the ponies, Ellie nodded. 'I'm just hoping Milly behaves herself.'

'Len'll murder you if she doesn't,' Luke said cheerfully. 'He was so mad last week.'

'Thanks. I do remember!'

Luke grinned. 'You'll be OK. Just remember "positive mental attitude". That's what you have to start off with.'

'Positive mental attitude,' Ellie repeated.

'You got it!' Luke's blue gaze met Ellie's. 'It'll be fine!'

Realizing it was nearly time for her class, Ellie went to change in the horsebox, swapping her old riding clothes for spotless yellow jodhpurs and a deep-brown tweed jacket. She coiled her blonde hair into a neat bun and tied her number round her waist. When she was done, she took a deep breath. This was it!

She returned to find Luke putting the finishing

touches to Milly for her, so she didn't dirty her show clothes. He was smoothing down the stray hairs around Milly's plaits and making sure her noseband was straight. 'She's ready. I'll be along to watch you when you go in,' he said, holding the stirrup as Ellie mounted. 'And remember, you *can* win this.'

'Thanks!' Ellie said gratefully. It was at moments like this when she liked Luke best – when he dropped the teasing act and was just like a normal person. No, not just a normal person, she realized, but someone who understood her love of competing. Taking a deep breath, she squeezed her heels against Milly's sides and headed over to the rings.

There were people everywhere – trainers talking to riders on horses, parents in tweed jackets, grooms carrying wicker baskets overflowing with brushes and cloths, lead-rein riders having their boots polished and red hair ribbons adjusted, and ponies being jumped over practice fences.

Ellie spotted her uncle, holding Fizz, with Veronica Armstrong standing beside him, dressed smartly in navy-blue with a matching hat. Emmie was with them, contentedly eating an ice cream. A red rosette hung on the string around Emmie's waist, the tails tucked neatly into her jacket pocket. She must have won her class and, judging by the 13 hands-high class that they were watching, Oliver was doing well too. He and Bill were standing third in the preliminary line-up. Len was smiling, his face approving for once.

'We'd better keep up the good work,' Ellie muttered to Milly.

She didn't feel like talking to the Armstrongs and so she warmed the pony up, keeping an eye on the ring. When the placings were announced, Oliver was moved up a place and presented with the blue second-place rosette. He looked very smug.

'Could have gone one better, but it's not bad,' Ellie heard her uncle say.

She walked Milly on. 'Hey, you!' Luke came striding over. Ellie saw how the girls riding in the working-in area all looked at him as he passed. 'How's it going?' he asked.

'OK, but I'd better keep her moving.'

Luke nodded. 'Just remember to get a killer gallop in – and don't go into the ring and follow the best pony like you did last week. Pick a donkey and follow that.'

Despite the jokey tone of his voice, Ellie knew it was good advice. 'OK.'

'You can win this class,' he told her. 'What have you got to remember?'

'Positive mental attitude?' Ellie said.

He grinned. 'Actually, I was going to say kick some ass!'

Ellie giggled, which instantly made her relax. A second later, the steward was calling her class in. 'Here we go,' she breathed to the pony, and clicking her tongue, she headed into the ring.

As Milly walked through the entrance, Ellie's shoulders moved back and she sat up straight. She loved being in the ring and she knew Milly did too. The chestnut pony walked energetically, her ears pricked, neck softly arched. Remembering Luke's advice from earlier, Ellie circled round to fit in behind a plain bay with a slightly coarse head. When all the competitors were in the ring, the steward asked them to trot, then canter on both reins, before they took it in turns to gallop down the long side of the ring. Ellie knew some riders worried about pushing on too hard in case they couldn't stop their pony at the end, but starting with a good gallop could really impress the judge, which was important in a class with as many good ponies as this one. She felt Milly's excitement as they cantered round in preparation; the pony knew what was coming. Ellie wondered whether to play safe and just let her go for a few strides before slowing down. But as she passed Luke at the ringside and saw him raise his eyebrows questioningly, she made up her mind. Playing safe wouldn't win the class. She'd rather risk getting into trouble than be careful.

Reaching the corner, she loosened her reins slightly, giving Milly her head and pushing on as hard as she could. The pony responded, thundering down the long side. Ellie had a worrying moment as they reached the corner and wondered if she would be able to stop, but she kept smiling and managed to bring Milly back to a canter, hoping it looked as if she was in perfect control.

Nailed it! she thought to herself with a leap of delight.

She glanced across at Luke. He clapped his hands loudly in approval and gave her a broad grin. She only just stopped herself from grinning back.

The judge also seemed impressed. Ellie was called in first. Each of the ponies would now do an individual show, so the judge could have a good look at them. After that, they would all untack and the judge would watch them walk and trot in-hand before making the final decisions on placing.

Ellie rode out and halted, smiling at the judge. All her practising that week paid off and Milly stood perfectly, four square, ears pricked. Ellie rode her away and began to trot in a figure of eight. The time flew by, Ellie finished with another thundering gallop and then brought the pony back to the judge, halted and bowed, before patting Milly hard and walking her back into her place. It had gone brilliantly! She watched the other ponies go and then it was time for the first ponies in the line to be untacked. Ellie's uncle came into the ring with a basket of grooming tools.

'Good work, lass,' he said as he started taking Milly's saddle off. Ellie just gave a brief nod. Since Merlin's death, her uncle's praise had meant nothing to her. But glancing across to the ringside, she saw Luke give her a big thumbs-up. That made her smile.

She stood by Milly's head, stroking her and talking as her uncle brushed her over, and then it was time to lead her out. Milly behaved perfectly.

Ellie held her breath as the steward was finally given the list of winners and started walking towards the line of ponies. Who would it be?

'Number one hundred and forty-two,' the judge called, pointing straight at her and Milly. Triumph swept through Ellie. They'd won!

The rosettes were given out and Ellie led the lap of honour round the ring. She cantered out to be met by Luke and her uncle. Len was smiling. 'Not bad riding, lass. Not bad riding at all.'

Luke met her with his hand raised in a high five. 'Way to go!'

Ellie smacked his hand with her own, then jumped off and hugged Milly fiercely. 'You were brilliant!' she told the mare.

Luke grinned. 'Told you, you could do it!'

Ellie glowed.

The rest of the day passed in a blur of activity. Ellie and Oliver Armstrong were both in the Show Hunter Pony Championships and, to Ellie's utter delight, Milly was chosen as the Champion. It was an amazing feeling to be presented with a massive rosette and have a sash placed round Milly's neck.

Luke completed the great day for the team by winning the Intermediate Championship on Zak, and then it was time to start the long drive home.

As they headed back on the motorway, Ellie found herself thinking about Spirit more and more. How was he? Had he eaten his feed that day? Joe had promised to make him a bran mash and stay with him while he was eating, to see if that helped.

Deep in the pit of her stomach she felt a gnawing, worried sensation. Horses didn't usually stop eating for no reason. She wanted to get back, stroke Spirit, talk to him, check he was all right.

By the time they reached the yard, it was almost dark. Joe came out of the house to help them unload and pack away.

'How's Spirit?' Ellie asked as she jumped down from the horsebox.

'He hasn't eaten much. I stayed with him while he ate, but it didn't seem to make much difference. Guess I'm not you.'

'Thanks for trying,' Ellie sighed.

Luke stretched and got out of the lorry. 'Get moving, you two. I'm out tonight.'

'You're going out?' It was nine o'clock, and after the long day with all the driving and the adrenalin of the show, Ellie was looking forward to collapsing on the sofa in front of the TV once the ponies were sorted.

Luke grinned. 'Of course. The night's not even begun yet and I have a hot date.'

Ellie shook her head. 'Why not wait until tomorrow to see Sasha?'

Luke grinned again. 'Who said anything about Sasha?'

Ellie fixed him with an unimpressed look. 'You're Sasha's boyfriend. You shouldn't be making a date with someone else.'

'And *you* really should live a bit more,' he told her. He turned and strode round the lorry to help Len who was starting to walk the ponies out.

She felt a rush of irritation and turned to Joe.

'So you had a good time at the show?' Joe asked as they took Fizz, Bill and Milly up to the barn.

Ellie nodded. 'It was great.' She told him all about her day as they put the ponies away, putting on their lightweight cotton rugs and feeding them.

'So what shall we do tonight?' Joe asked as they finally finished and fastened the stable doors.

'Watch some TV?' said Ellie.

'Sounds good to me,' Joe agreed. 'There's pizza to eat too.'

Ellie smiled. Just what she felt like – pizza and TV with Joe. 'Can I just see Spirit first?'

'Sure.'

But as she turned to leave him, Len appeared in the barn door, his figure silhouetted against the darkness outside. 'You two are taking your time here. What's going on?' Ellie blinked as she heard the faint note of accusation in his voice.

'Nothing, we're just finishing the ponies off,' she said in surprise.

'Are they done?'

'Yes,' Joe replied.

'I was just going to see Spirit,' said Ellie.

Len looked from her to Joe, then back to her again. 'Go on then,' he grunted. She felt his eyes watching as she walked past him. Why was he being so weird? Suddenly she remembered how he'd caught her holding Joe's hands the day before and her eyes widened. Surely he didn't think there was something going on between them? It would certainly explain why he'd given them such an accusing look just now. But if he was thinking that, he was so wrong. Shaking her head, Ellie felt glad that she and Joe *had* decided they were just friends.

Letting herself into Spirit's stable, Ellie put her

arms round his neck and pushed aside thoughts of her uncle.

Spirit breathed out softly, his muzzle exploring her face.

Ellie shut her eyes. Even though their minds weren't connected, she could feel the energy that swirled through him. She frowned slightly, something about his energy was different from how it used to be. She couldn't put her finger on it, but it felt as if the force flowing was jagged somehow, uneven not smooth.

Pushing aside her own tiredness, she moved her hands lightly over his body, focusing on the strange feelings and letting herself explore the sensation. She'd never felt anything like it. What did it mean?

She moved to his head and let her mind open to his.

Is there something wrong with you? she asked anxiously.

A feeling of reassurance flowed from him. She had a strong impression that he was telling her not to worry.

But you're not eating and something feels wrong, she said to him. *Can't I do anything?*

No. Do not worry. He sent her a picture of the show, asking what she had been doing.

She told him all about the day, about winning the class and how the other horses and ponies had done.

Spirit listened. Finally, she gave a yawn, becoming aware how tired she really was. She let the connection fade and kissed his forehead, feeling love swelling through her. 'I'm going in now. See you in the morning,' she whispered.

Her eyes fell on his ribs. Spirit might say there was nothing to worry about, but why wasn't he eating and why was she picking up these strange sensations? Trying to ignore the anxiety twisting through her, she left his stable and went into the farmhouse for the night.

Chapter Three

Ellie couldn't concentrate the next day at school. Spirit had only eaten about a third of his feed that morning. Even though she had been with him, he had turned away, uninterested, after a few mouthfuls. It just wasn't like him. But when she had spoken to him about it, he'd told her once again that he was all right and said he would like to go out for a ride that evening. Surely he wouldn't have wanted to do that if he was feeling ill?

As Mr Henson, her maths teacher, droned on about tangents and cosines, Ellie thought about how she could fit everything in. Milly would be having a day off, but she would have to ride Gem and Picasso. Maybe after that, though, she could take Spirit out into the woods.

'Ellie, perhaps you can tell me the answer?'

Ellie jumped guiltily as Mr Henson approached her desk. She went red, not having a clue what the question was.

'Um . . . I . . .'

The teacher fixed her with a look. 'If you can't pay attention in my class, then you'll have to pay attention after school during detention.'

'Sorry,' Ellie muttered. To her relief, Mr Henson moved on, choosing one of the others to answer the question on the board.

Ellie sighed and forced herself to listen. The last thing she wanted was a detention and even less time to see Spirit!

Joe was on study leave from school because of his exams, so Ellie travelled back on the school bus alone. She hadn't made many real friends at school. It was hard joining when you were fourteen and in Year Ten. Most of the time she kept her head down and just wished each day to be over.

When she got off the bus, she saw Luke in Len's car, waiting to drive her back. Sasha was in the front with him. As Ellie came nearer, she frowned. Sasha looked furious and seemed to be shouting at Luke. He was rolling his eyes.

'Hi,' Ellie said, opening the back door.

Luke smiled, but Sasha didn't even turn round. 'But you kissed her!' she hissed at Luke, obviously not wanting Ellie to hear. 'My friend Lucy's just texted me – she said she saw you with her. Don't deny it!'

'OK, so I kissed her. It's no big deal.' Luke shrugged.

'No big deal? We're supposed to be going out, Luke!' Sasha threw herself back angrily against the seat.

Luke started the engine. He held the steering wheel easily with one hand and turned the music on with the other. Catching Ellie's eye in the mirror, he made an apologetic face.

She frowned back at him, refusing to let him think he could get away with behaving like that. Ellie didn't particularly like Sasha, but right now she felt sorry for her having Luke as a boyfriend.

They drove home with only the music to break the silence. When they arrived, Sasha shut the car door with a bang and stomped away. Luke watched her go, shaking his head. 'Sorry about that.'

Ellie looked at him pointedly. 'But you're not sorry for kissing whoever it was.'

'Anna Hallett as it happens – and nope, I'm not.'

'Anna Hallett!' Ellie gaped. Anna Hallett was Lucifer's owner, and the daughter of one of Len's biggest sponsor's, Jeff Hallett. Jeff's company Equi-Glow paid for all the horse feed at High Peak Stables and Len had warned Luke to keep away from Anna Hallett as it might affect the sponsorship deal if he upset her. 'Anna Hallett!' she repeated, picturing the very beautiful dark-haired nineteen-year-old.

Luke nodded. 'I saw her at the show on Thursday that Lucifer went to. We thought we'd hook up last night – and we did.'

'Luke!' Ellie stared at him. 'Len will be totally mad and Sasha is really upset.'

'Len will never know and Sasha'll get over it,' Luke said, sounding supremely unbothered. 'It's not as if Sasha and I are that serious. I'm not hearing wedding bells with her, you know.'

'But you shouldn't treat people like that. You really shouldn't. It's wrong!'

Luke's mouth quirked into a grin. 'You're telling me off?'

'Someone has to!' Ellie responded sharply.

Luke chuckled and walked away. With a sigh of exasperation, Ellie went into the house to get changed.

Ellie's bedroom was on the top floor, while Joe, Luke and Len all had rooms on the first floor. She changed her clothes and headed back downstairs. Joe looked out of his bedroom as she passed.

'Hey there.'

'How come you're inside?' she asked.

'I thought I'd do some work while Dad's out. You know what he's like – study leave to him just means I'll have more time to work the horses.'

Ellie couldn't imagine choosing to do school work instead of being outside. 'But why are you bothering to revise? It's not as if you're staying on at school and need good grades.' Joe's GCSE exams were in a few weeks' time and after he had done them he would leave school to work on the yard full time. She wished she was as old as him, but she still had another year at school. It wasn't her birthday until the end of July.

'I know, but I still want to do as well as I can,' said Joe.

Ellie shook her head. It was typical of him. He was so different from her. He reminded her of her dad in many ways.

'I'd better get on. I think Dad's planning on being back by five with Ray.'

'Who's Ray?' Ellie asked.

'Ray's an old friend of Dad's. He used to produce show horses like Dad, then he moved to Canada. He and Dad have kept in touch. Dad really respects him. He has some massive stables out there and is doing really well.' Joe stretched. 'OK, work time for me. When this is finished I need to ride Wisp. We could go out for a hack on him and Spirit after I've schooled him if you feel like it.'

'Definitely!' Ellie hurried on down the stairs and went to bring Spirit in from the field. White clouds were floating across the blue sky and the warm summer air smelt of grass and horses. Honeysuckle and dog roses scrambled through the hedges that bordered the path down to the fields, and in the nearby trees she could hear the birds calling to each other. She breathed in happily. She loved early summer when everything was growing and fresh.

Climbing the metal gate, she spotted Spirit. He seemed to be watching for her because even before she called his name he was trotting over. He coughed as he stopped, and she frowned as she saw his ribs move under his skin.

'Oh, Spirit, you really do need to eat more,' she said as he pushed his nose against her chest. She stroked his grey face, noticing that he'd been bitten by flies – there were little lumps on his chest. 'I should have put fly repellant on you,' she said, cross with herself for forgetting. 'Have the flies been bothering you? Come on, let's get you in.'

Sasha and Helen were in the tackroom. Ellie could hear Sasha's voice as she reached the yard.

'I can't believe he kissed her! He didn't even say sorry!'

'It's awful, I know, but that's what Luke's like,' Helen's softer voice said.

'Do you think he's seeing her?'

'I don't know. Maybe it was just a one-off thing.'

'I bet he's arranged to meet up with her again,' Sasha said angrily.

Ellie tried to block out the voices. Whatever was going on was none of her business. She concentrated on Spirit instead, brushing him over, talking to him all the while.

She was just finishing off when Luke came to find her. 'Have you time to look at Gabriel, Ellie? I think there's something up with him. He's been fighting the bit and throwing his head around the last few days. You might be able to figure out what's wrong with him for me.'

Ellie hesitated. She was still feeling cross with him and was tempted to say no, but she pushed aside the irritation. A horse needed helping and, after all, as she'd just thought, Luke's love life was absolutely no concern of hers. 'OK.'

'Thanks. He's in his stable, should I take him up to the school for you?'

'No, I'll have a look at him in his stable first. Give me ten minutes on my own with him.'

Luke looked surprised. 'Why? What are you going to do?'

'I just need some time with him. Can you put Spirit's grooming kit away for me?' Not waiting for an answer, Ellie left him standing there and went to Gabriel's stable.

The big bay gelding gave her a curious look as

she went in. He was a confident and friendly horse who liked people. His eyes were alert and interested. He came over to Ellie as if wondering what she was doing there, his muzzle searching her pockets for treats. Ellie rubbed his forehead. 'Hi, boy.'

He accepted the fuss, and then when he was sure she didn't have a treat for him, he turned away. Ellie stood back against the stable wall. She had to relax, gradually tuning into his energy and waiting to see if he would talk. Shutting her eyes, she let all the other thoughts that were filling her brain fade away. This was always the hardest bit for her – she was such an active person, never still. It was an effort to just stand quietly, thinking about the horse, breathing and waiting. As she breathed in and out, she gradually became aware of the energy pulsing through Gabriel.

Do you want to talk? she thought to him. There was silence in the stable, he wasn't moving in the straw and he had stopped eating his hay. *I'm here if you want to speak to me. I'll listen. I want to know if you're all right.*

Ellie felt a flicker of impatience when he didn't reply, but she pushed it away. Spirit had taught her that she must offer to listen and then wait, be patient.

She sent all the love she could to the horse. *I just want to help.*

Suddenly she felt it, a change in the atmosphere, a connection opening. *Gabriel?*

Yes.

She opened her eyes. The big bay was staring at her. *I can hear you,* she thought.

His nostrils quivered in a faint acknowledgement. She felt as if his dark intelligent eyes were absorbing her, drawing her in. She walked over and touched his neck. *Tell me what's wrong . . .*

Ellie lost track of how long she was speaking to Gabriel, but eventually she sensed he'd had enough. *Thank you,* she told him and, with a shake of her head, she stepped back and let the connection close.

'You finished yet?' She jumped as she heard Luke's voice and, swinging round, saw him looking over the stable door. 'What are you doing?' he said curiously.

'Just being with him.'

'Talking to him? Doing your horse-whispering stuff you mean?'

'It's not like that. Anyway, I know what's wrong with him,' she said, changing the subject and patting Gabriel. The horse pushed against her.

'Really?'

Ellie nodded. 'He's bored. You're just schooling him in the same old routine time after time.' The bay horse had been very clear in his thoughts about how fed up he was with Luke always repeating the same movements. Luke wasn't really into schooling, preferring jumping, hacking out and showing. He saw the everyday schooling they did as a chore. 'It's why he's started being resistant, ducking out and avoiding the bit. He just wants a change.'

'But you haven't even seen me riding him. How can you possibly know that?'

Ellie's eyes met the horse's. 'I just do. Oh . . .' She turned back to Luke. 'And he doesn't like you riding with your mobile phone. He doesn't like the buzz it makes when it rings – he can feel it down the reins.' She hid her smile at Luke's stunned face. She was telling the truth; it was what Gabriel had said to her, but she could understand Luke's astonishment.

'My mobile phone . . .' He trailed off and grinned. 'OK, nice one, Ellie! You almost got me there!'

'No, I mean it, Luke. You can't ride him with it,' insisted Ellie. 'Not if you want him to go better. Trust me. Take him up to the school, don't have your mobile and ride some different schooling exercises to see.'

Luke stared at her for a moment, then shrugged. 'OK, why not? It's crazy-mad but what's to lose?'

Ellie smiled to herself as he collected the tack and dumped his phone in the tackroom. That was the good thing about Luke – he was always ready to try things out. He never saw the arguments for why something shouldn't be done; he just did it.

Ten minutes later, they were up in the school, with Luke riding round Ellie as she stood in the centre. She knew exactly the routine of schooling exercises he usually did on Gabriel because Gabriel had sent her pictures of them, along with feelings of intense boredom. 'OK, instead of doing lots of circles and serpentines, work on his transitions today,' Ellie called. 'Mix things up, make it interesting – ride the corners, rectangles.'

Luke grinned, amused. 'You know, I do like it when you're strict, Ellie.'

Ellie fixed him with a look. 'Just do it!'

Focusing on the horse, Luke began to ride Gabriel through the different transitions – walk to trot, trot to canter, back down to walk, trot to halt and walk to canter. Gabriel worked nicely, looking alert and responsive. 'He's going well,' said Luke in surprise. 'I'll try some lateral work.'

He began to add in leg yielding, turns on the forehand and turns on the haunches.

'Try some circles now,' encouraged Ellie. 'But leg yield out so they gradually get bigger rather than just going round and round.'

The two of them were utterly focused on the horse, and by the time they had finished, Gabriel was moving beautifully. Luke brought him to a halt, patting him. 'That was so much better. Thanks.' He dismounted. 'I don't know how you worked out what was wrong but it's made a massive difference. I can't believe it was as simple as him being bored.'

Ellie smiled. 'And not liking your mobile!'

'Maybe a change in ring tone?' Luke said, his eyes teasing. 'I could try out different ones and see if there's one he likes –'

'No mobile!' Ellie laughed. However much she disliked his behaviour to Sasha, it was difficult to be angry with Luke for long.

They led Gabriel out of the school and down to the courtyard, but just as they reached it, Sasha came marching out of the tackroom. 'What's this?' she demanded, thrusting Luke's mobile angrily at him. 'You're planning on meeting Anna again, tomorrow night? So were you going to tell me?'

Luke looked outraged. 'You've been reading my texts!'

'Yeah. And lucky I did. It's over, Luke. Totally over. You're dumped!' Sasha threw the phone down on the ground and stormed off.

For a moment, there was silence.

'Here, I'll take Gabriel. You go after her,' Ellie said.

'Go after her? No way.' Luke chucked the reins

at Ellie and went to pick up his phone, checking it for damage.

'Luke, she's upset and so she should be! You've been arranging to meet Anna behind her back!'

Luke shrugged. 'It's no big deal. It was fun while it lasted but it's been two months now.' He took Gabriel from Ellie and led him to his stable.

Ellie went after him. 'And that's a long time, is it?'

'For me!' he called over his shoulder.

Exasperation surged up inside her. She marched to the stable door. Luke was untacking Gabriel, patting him. As Ellie looked at him, caring for the horse, she felt herself falter, her anger fading a notch.

Luke saw her face. 'Ellie,' he half pleaded. 'Don't be mad with me. It's not as if Sasha and I were engaged. I'm not the type to settle down with one girl. I've never pretended otherwise.'

Ellie paused. 'Don't you ever want to have a serious girlfriend?'

'I don't do serious.' Luke shrugged again. 'If someone wants serious, they should go out with someone else.'

His gaze flicked to the farmhouse, to Joe's bedroom window. 'So what about you? I thought for a while . . . you and Joe?'

'No!' Ellie said quickly. 'No, no! Not me and Joe. We're just friends.'

Luke didn't speak for a few moments, taking off the brushing boots that Gabriel wore to protect his legs when he was being worked. 'Has Len said anything about it?'

'No.' Ellie stared at him. 'Why?'

'It's just I have a feeling he thinks there might be something going on.'

'Going on!' Ellie frowned. 'But that's stupid! That's –'

Luke held up his hands. 'Hey, don't shoot the messenger. I just thought you'd better know.'

'What's he said?' Ellie demanded.

'A few things in the last day or so, about watching you two carefully. Yesterday, he asked me if I thought there was anything between you.'

'Oh, great,' Ellie groaned, pushing a hand through her long hair.

'If there's nothing happening, then you haven't got a problem,' Luke pointed out, heaving the saddle off Gabriel's back and plonking it in her arms. 'Right, all done. Thanks for helping.'

'No problem. And, Luke?'

'Yeah?'

'Thanks for the warning about Uncle Len.'

'Any time.'

Ellie took the saddle to the tackroom, her thoughts going over what Luke had just said.

She decided to forget it; if her uncle wanted to

be suspicious that was his problem. There were too many other things for her to think about – like Spirit not eating – without worrying about her uncle too. *He'll forget about it soon*, she thought.

Chapter Four

By the time Ellie had ridden Gem and Picasso, Joe had come out of the house. She met him in the pony barn, tacking Wisp up. 'Luke's just told me about you helping him with Gabriel. How did you work out what was wrong with him?'

'I just guessed.'

'But how?' Joe insisted. 'You're amazing. You just do these things – you got Picasso to load when no one else could, you worked out Troy had hurt his back, realized Lucifer needed to be ridden really gently, and now you've sorted Gabriel out too. How *do* you work these things out?'

Ellie remembered her decision to tell him the truth. Maybe now was the right time. 'Well,' she said carefully, watching his reaction. 'It is a bit weird, but I talk to them and they talk back. I can hear them in my head.'

Joe grinned. 'Yeah, right.'

'No, it happens.'

'Come on, Els. Tell me the truth! How do you work it out?'

Ellie gave up. She didn't blame Joe for not believing it; if she hadn't experienced it herself she'd have found it hard to accept. She sighed, falling back on her old story. 'It's like I told you before – I'm just good at guessing.'

'So it's all about intuition?'

'Yeah.'

Joe nodded. Intuition was something he could understand. 'Well, I think it's really cool. Could you help me, do you think? Wisp's been coming off the track when I'm riding him. Will you come and watch him? Maybe you can work out why he's doing it.'

'It doesn't quite work like that,' Ellie answered. 'But I'll come and watch.' She wondered whether to tell him what Luke had said about Len but decided not to. She and Joe hadn't talked like that since they'd decided nothing would happen between them, and she didn't want to start an awkward conversation.

Luke was working Lucifer in the main ménage now, so Ellie and Joe took Wisp to the small schooling ring by the car park.

Wisp was a beautiful 14.3 hands-high dun pony, with a coat the colour of pale sand and a jet-black mane and tail. Joe competed him in the 15 hands-high show hunter pony classes. It was only Wisp's second season of showing. He was very handsome but not an easy ride, being stubborn and sometimes lazy, but Joe always stayed patient and Wisp usually worked well for him. Now Joe worked him on a loose rein, encouraging his head to come down as he moved forward, his back and neck rounding softly. Gradually, Joe shortened Wisp's reins, so he went into more of an outline, all the time moving him forwards, encouraging him to stay relaxed and obedient.

Ellie leant against the gate. She loved watching Joe ride. He was so quiet in the saddle, so sensitive to how the horse was moving. Luke was a brilliant rider too, but a totally different type, naturally stronger and more forceful, he was particularly good with the bolder, stronger horses on the yard.

'Do you see what he's doing?' Joe called to Ellie as he rode Wisp down one of the long sides of the school and Wisp drifted in off the track instead of trotting perfectly straight. 'I can stop him if I use my inside leg really hard, but I have to do that every single time.' He drew the dun pony to a halt. 'I'm not sure why he's doing it. Any ideas?'

But Ellie couldn't help. She knew if she'd been alone with Wisp and able to talk to him, she could ask him why he was coming off the track, but she couldn't answer Joe's question there and then. 'Sorry. I haven't a clue.'

'He doesn't feel tense or upset,' mused Joe. 'He's not spooking at anything or scared of something by the fence. It's almost as if he simply doesn't feel like going on the track so he's not –'

He broke off as his dad drove into the car park.

'Here's Dad and Ray.'

The car stopped and the two men got out. Ray was a tall slim man in his fifties, with deeply tanned skin, wearing jeans and a Stetson hat over his grey hair. He lifted his hand in greeting. 'Hey there, Joe!'

'Hi!' Joe called back.

Ray walked over with Len. As he came closer, Ellie saw that his eyes were sky-blue and friendly. He smiled at her. 'You're Len's niece, right?' His voice was a strange mix – a hint of Derbyshire but with a Canadian twang, his words lifting up slightly at the end of each sentence. 'I'm Ray Jones. Pleased to meet you.' He held out his hand.

'I'm Ellie. Hi.'

'That sure is a nice-looking pony,' Ray commented, giving Wisp an appreciative look.

'That's Wisp,' said Len, joining them. 'Qualified for HOYS last year in his first season but behaved like a bugger in the ring. Nice to look at but not easy. We'll get there with him, though. He just needs time to grow up.' He glanced at Joe. 'Show Ray what he can do then.'

Joe rode off, moving Wisp into a trot and then a canter. He circled in a figure of eight, then round the school, lengthening the pony's stride.

Ray watched. 'Moves like a dream, but he's coming off the track a bit,' he commented.

Len nodded. 'Get that inside leg on properly, Joe.'

Joe trotted round again and this time used his inside leg even harder against the pony's side to keep him on the track. Wisp's ears immediately went back and his head came up in complaint.

'Bloody hell!' Len muttered.

'I've got an idea.' Ray glanced at Len. 'May I?'

'Be my guest,' said Len, to Ellie's surprise. He usually hated anyone interfering with his horses.

Letting himself into the ring, Ray went up to the pony and patted him. He studied him for a few moments and then spoke to Joe. 'Is he stiff? Do you think he could be hurting anywhere?'

'No, I don't have that feeling at all. Apart from that one spot on the track, he's working really well.'

'In that case, it's my guess he's just deciding he'll do what he wants, not what you want him to do. I think you can learn a lot from a horse's face and his tells me he's a stubborn guy. You see the way his face dishes in here.' Ray ran his hand down Wisp's nose. 'And comes out in a slight bump between the eyes, then out again here in a moose nose. I've often found that horses with faces like this have a difficult nature; I'd say Wisp likes to call the shots. His long mouth and a long, narrow flat chin also suggest to me he's a horse who likes doing what he wants – and not what the rider wants.'

'You've just described him perfectly!' said Joe, glancing at Ellie. It was Wisp down to a tee.

'I've worked with quite a few horses like this,' said Ray, stepping back and looking Wisp all over. 'Sure, you can bully them into doing what you want, but if you do that you'll never be able to trust them because sure as hell they'll get back at you one day – usually when you're in the ring for the big performance. What you need to do is persuade them to work with you.'

'How do you do that?' Ellie was intrigued.

Ray's blue eyes met hers. 'By giving them a choice – not forcing them, make it easy for them to do what you want, hard but not impossible for them to do what they want. There's almost no horse so stubborn he'll choose to work twice as hard just to have his own way.'

'I know that kind of stuff!' Joe burst out. 'I've been reading about it in books.'

Len snorted. 'He fancies himself as some kind of horse-whisperer. Been doing that joining-up nonsense.'

Ray shook his head. 'It's not nonsense, Len. You're

behind the times. I use it to start all my youngsters off.' He turned to Joe. 'Good on you, son,' he said approvingly.

Ellie shot a look at her uncle; for once he looked as if he didn't know quite what to say.

'So, you've been reading about this, apply what you know to the situation,' Ray focused on Joe. 'You want this pony to go along the track, he wants to come off. What are you going to do about it?'

Joe thought for a second. 'Let him come off the track?' he said at last. 'But make it harder work for him if he does?'

Ray smiled. 'Got it in one. Every time he tries to come off, let him do that but circle him round, a nice tight ten-metre circle, and don't let him stop until he's been round five times, then he can come back on the track. The second he steps off, you let him, but if he's coming off he's gonna circle. Got it?'

'Got it,' said Joe eagerly. He clicked his tongue and rode off.

Ray walked back to the gate and smiled at Len. 'There are more ways to get horses to do what you want than just by forcing them,' he said. 'I've been learning that a lot these last few years.'

Len shook his head. 'Maybe with the eventers you're dealing with now. But show horses – they need to be a hundred per cent obedient, do what they're told when they're told.'

'Get a partnership with a horse, so it feels it's working with you not for you, and it doesn't matter what area you're competing in – jumping, eventing, showing. You'll see the difference,' Ray said, adjusting his hat.

Ellie was fascinated to watch the relationship between the two men. She'd never seen her uncle with someone he clearly respected before.

Joe was turning Wisp down the long side of the school. This time, as the pony came off the track, instead of clamping his inside leg against the pony's side, Joe let him come off the track but rode him into a small fast circle as Ray had suggested. He went round five times and then came back to the track. Wisp looked decidedly surprised. He went on a few more paces and then tried creeping in again. Joe did exactly as he had done before. It took three times round the ring, but suddenly Wisp seemed to understand the rules – if he trotted on the track, he could go straight and it was nice and easy for him; if he tried to come off, Joe would make him circle, which was difficult and uncomfortable. On the fourth time round, Wisp stayed beautifully on the track all the time, his neck arched, his strides loose and free.

'And bring him to a stop!' Ray said as Joe patted the pony. 'You did it!'

'It worked!' Joe's face was glowing.

'You did great. Stayed calm and patient. That's the

key. Don't get angry or het up – just give a horse the choice and wait for it to realize it's better to do what *you* want.'

Joe looked delighted.

'Joe's really patient,' Ellie couldn't resist saying, pleased that at last someone was telling him how good he was. 'He's brilliant with the young horses.'

Ray looked at Joe. 'I'd give you a job any day, son. Stick with the natural horsemanship and don't let your dad talk you out of it. It works.' He turned to Len. 'You'll see that in the end.'

'Bloody hell,' said Len, but he spoke in a good-humoured way. 'You and your new ways. You coming to see the rest of the yard then? It's grown a bit since you were last here. There are two new barns for a start. Joe, take Wisp down the drive to cool him off.'

The two men walked off together, talking.

'Wow! Isn't Ray brilliant?' Ellie burst out when they were out of earshot.

'Awesome!' said Joe. 'And he was so right to do that with Wisp.'

'It was like the work you did with Milly the other day.' Ellie beamed at him. 'Joe! He thought you were really good. Isn't that great?'

Joe seemed lost for words; he nodded and grinned.

'He said he'd even give you a job!' Ellie looked at him. 'Maybe you could ask him for one? You'd learn loads if you worked for him.'

She held her breath. Would Joe really consider it? She hoped not. She couldn't imagine life on the yard without him.

To her relief, he shook his head. 'Don't be daft. It would be amazing, of course it would, and I'd love to work on a yard that was into join-up and stuff. But you know Dad would never let me leave here. Still, it's cool that Ray said that.'

'Very cool,' Ellie agreed.

She tacked Spirit up, then she and Joe set out into the woods. Now the heat of the day was fading it was the perfect temperature for riding. The sun slanted down through the trees, casting shadows on the dry ground. They rode in the shade of the woods, taking it slowly because Ellie didn't want to push Spirit too hard. She hadn't been sure about riding him, but when she'd taken the tack into his stable he'd almost pushed his head into the bridle, as if eager to be out.

They rode out of the woods and on to the higher slopes of the mountains, sticking to the bridle paths along the field edges. Sheep baaed and overhead the occasional bird of prey hovered. It was a wild land-scape with the sharp tops of the mountains outlined against the blue sky, the grey walls falling down in places, strands of barbed wire strung along the top, and orange bale-string holding gates closed.

When Ellie had first started riding up there, Joe

had warned her to stick to the paths and watch the weather carefully. It could change from bright sunshine to mist very quickly so it was easy to get lost up on the mountainside, or for a horse to stumble on uneven ground and lame itself badly.

'You have to be so careful,' he'd warned. 'There are all sorts of dangers up here.'

Ellie had found out he was right just a few weeks ago. She'd been trying to persuade Spirit through a gap in a stone wall, but he just kept refusing. In the end, she'd tried to lead him through and discovered some sharp and rusty strands of lethal barbed wire tangled in the long grass. If Spirit had walked through them, they would have tangled around his legs and injured him badly. Remembering it now as they rode alongside a crumbling wall, she leant forward and gave him a hug. He always looked after her whatever they were doing.

They stopped near the top of a peak and looked down across the valley. They could see High Peak Stables clinging to the mountainside, the horses looking like toys in the fields. Further down in the valley was the town. It all looked so wonderfully far away. Ellie breathed in the clear mountain air. There was no place she would rather be. Being out here, like this, with Spirit and Joe, free from being watched and being shouted at, everything felt right with the world.

'We must come out on rides more,' she said dreamily.

'Yeah,' Joe agreed. 'When you break up from school we might be able to take half a day or something, with a picnic. There are loads of brilliant rides – we'll have to make the most of the summer.'

Spirit put his head down and coughed twice.

Ellie felt a shiver of foreboding. Would Spirit be well enough for picnic rides? She forced the thought away. Of course he would be. He was just a bit off colour right now. She would find out what was wrong and sort it out. She could feel how happy Spirit was to be out on the mountains. He'd be fine.

She looked up at a sparrow hawk hovering above them in the sky, then leant down and hugged Spirit, resting her cheek against his neck.

Chapter Five

When Ellie and Joe got back, Len and Ray were chatting on the yard. As Joe led Wisp up to the pony barn, Ray came over to Ellie. 'So this is your horse?'

Ellie nodded. 'I bought him at a sale.'

'Len told me about that.' Ray held out his hand and let Spirit sniff him. To Ellie's surprise, Spirit nuzzled him. He was usually wary of strangers, particularly men but he instantly seemed to take to Ray. 'Hey, fella.' Ray's eyes ran over the scars on Spirit's shoulder and legs. 'Looks like he's had a tough life.'

'He was badly treated in his last two homes,' Ellie explained. Spirit had shared with her all his memories of the different homes he had been at.

Ray walked around Spirit, and Ellie noticed that Spirit stood quietly, unusually relaxed. Ray offered him his hand again. 'Is it all right if I stroke you?' he said as if asking Spirit's permission.

'He doesn't normally like new people,' Ellie put in quickly.

But to her surprise Spirit didn't move as Ray laid one hand on his neck and another on his back. A frown slowly deepened on Ray's tanned face.

'Hmm,' he said, half in thought.

'What is it?' Ellie asked anxiously.

'Have you noticed him being off colour at all?'

'Yes, actually, I have. He's not been eating and he's been quieter than normal and he has been coughing.'

'Maybe best to get him checked out by the vet.' Ray felt under Spirit's cheeks and jaw and on his chest. 'His glands are up a bit. And you want to get these little lumps checked out.'

'Aren't they just fly bites?' Ellie said.

'Maybe. Maybe not. Get the vet to look at them.'

'I will.' Ellie felt worried.

'It may be nothing,' Ray went on. 'It's just I've got some experience in sensing horses' energy fields and his feels wrong.'

'I know!' Ellie caught herself as he looked at her in surprise. 'I mean, I kind of sensed there was something wrong with him . . . What do you mean you've trained in sensing horses' energy fields?' she probed.

'All living creatures have an energy field around them and energy running through them – when they're ill or upset then the energy is blocked or distorted. You can train yourself to feel it. Some people are gifted and can feel it naturally; others like me need to learn how to do it. Everyone is capable of it though – if they learn to listen to their intuition.' Ray looked at her. 'Len says you're good with the horses – that you seem to have a bit of a knack for guessing what's wrong with them.'

'Yes.' Ellie's heart was beating fast. She'd never heard anyone talking about the sensations she got before. Ray was making it sound normal. 'I can sense things about horses, feel things.' She didn't want to say more with the others nearby.

Ray smiled. 'You're probably using your intuition without even realizing it. Maybe you're one of the gifted ones.'

Ellie longed to ask more, but Ray was already turning and patting Spirit. 'Sorry, fella. We're standing here talking and you must want to be back in your stall.' He glanced round at Ellie. 'Do get him checked out.'

'I will.'

She took Spirit back to his stable, worry running through her. If she and Ray could both sense there was something wrong, then there must be. She gently touched the lumps on Spirit's chest. If they weren't fly bites, what were they?

'You'll be OK,' she told him firmly. Giving him a kiss, she left him to his haynet.

Joe was in the tackroom. 'So what was Ray saying to you about Spirit?' he asked as she hung up the bridle.

'He thinks I should get him checked out by the vet.'

Joe gave her a comforting look. 'Spirit's probably just got a virus or something. He doesn't look sick – just a bit skinny.'

Ellie nodded. Joe was right; she knew there were lots of different viruses that horses could get. They weren't usually very serious.

'He'll be fine,' Joe said firmly. 'Now, come on, Dad was talking about a barbecue.'

Len and Ray started a barbecue in the little garden behind the farmhouse, while Ellie and Joe fetched plates, bread rolls and salad. Luke had gone out for the night so it was just the four of them. Ellie was struck by how different her uncle was with Ray there – much more relaxed. The two men sat in deckchairs, laughing about old times and things they'd got up to when they were young and on the showing circuit together. Joe sat down on the swing seat next to Ellie.

The talk moved on to Canada and Ray showed them pictures of his large stables there. It looked amazing, set in the Rocky Mountains, three white barns with red roofs and pasture all around.

'I never thought I'd see the day – you into all this horse-whispering stuff,' said Len, shaking his head.

'You should try it, Len. I imagine Joe here could teach you – or Ellie. I think she's got a talent.' Ray smiled at them both. 'They're great kids. You're very lucky.'

'Do you have children?' Ellie asked him.

'No. My wife, Sarah, and I wanted to but it never happened. But that's the way it goes. You can't plan what life will hold for you.' He turned to Len. 'Did you hear that Bob Anderson died last week?'

'Bob?'

Ray nodded. 'It was a massive heart attack. And he was only our age. No one found out about it for two days.'

Len sucked the air in through his teeth. 'Poor sod.'

Ray glanced at Ellie and Joe. 'Bob used to ride in the ring with us when we were younger. Gave up the riding to concentrate on having a stud farm, though, about ten years ago.'

'I sold him a really nice working hunter mare I retired last year,' said Len.

'Fern?' asked Joe.

Len nodded. 'She had a great jump. Bob bred her to a warmblood stallion. The foal was due a few weeks ago. So what's happening to all the horses?'

'They're being sold – that's what I heard today, anyway,' said Ray.

Len rubbed his mouth thoughtfully. 'I might ring up and see if they've still got her. She's a lovely mare and I'd like to see the foal she's produced.'

'Will you buy them?' Joe asked.

'Might do.'

Ray stretched and stood up. 'Well, I'd best be

getting back to my hotel if you're all right to give me a lift, Len. You two take care of yourselves,' he said to Joe and Ellie. 'And any time either of you fancy a trip to Canada just give me a ring or drop me an email. You're more than welcome to come and stay. I hope that grey of yours is OK, Ellie.'

'Thanks.'

They said goodbye and Len and Ray left.

A few minutes later, Ellie heard the car engine start up. 'I wish Ray could stay for longer. He's amazing.'

Joe nodded. 'There's so much more I'd like to ask him. He knows loads. He's done Parelli training and T-Touch and been on a course with Monty Roberts.'

'Do you think your dad will start taking things like join-up more seriously?' Ellie said hopefully.

Joe snorted. 'Don't be daft. It'll be business as usual in the morning.'

Ellie sighed, knowing he was right. It would take more than one visit from an old friend to change her uncle's ingrained ways. She began to swing the seat.

For a while neither of them spoke; the evening grew darker around them as the seat creaked in the still night. 'We should clear up in a minute,' Joe said with a sigh.

'Mmm.' Suddenly Ellie was struggling to keep her eyes open – it had been a long day. She rested her head against Joe's shoulder. 'I'm tired,' she said, with a yawn.

'Me too,' agreed Joe, putting his head back and shutting his eyes. The seat creaked gently and swung on . . .

'What the bloody hell!'

Ellie woke with a start at the sound of her uncle's loud voice. Her eyes blinked open and she realized she and Joe had fallen asleep on the swing seat, with her head on his chest. They jumped apart as if someone had tipped scalding water over them.

'What's going on here?' Len's voice was harsh, his eyes angry.

'What? N-nothing!' stammered Ellie, remembering the conversation with Luke and realizing what he was thinking.

'We just fell asleep, Dad,' Joe said, looking confused.

Len's eyes narrowed. 'You fell asleep together?'

'Yes, it was the swing. We were tired. That's all. We'd meant to clear up –' Joe broke off and Ellie saw the realization dawn on him as he looked into his father's angry eyes. 'No!' he said suddenly, getting up. 'There's nothing going on – nothing like that. Honestly!'

'There'd better not be,' Len ground out. He stepped closer to Joe, his whole body tense. 'Or you'll be sorry.'

'There isn't! There –'

'Tidy this mess up!' Len snapped.

Heart pounding, Ellie started to help Joe stack the plates and pick up glasses. Len watched them, his eyes still narrowed. He didn't leave them alone again but followed them into the kitchen. He waited until they had finished stacking the dishwasher and clearing the rubbish.

'I'm going to my room,' Ellie said as soon as everything was done.

Len gave a brief nod and Ellie thankfully escaped up the stairs. She couldn't believe she and Joe had fallen asleep together like that. Now her uncle would be even more suspicious. *But what can he do?* she thought. *Nothing's happening, so there's nothing for him to stop.*

However, even as she thought that, she knew she didn't trust her uncle.

Trying to forget about it, she changed into her pyjamas, but as she got into bed she was unable to completely wipe the sense of foreboding from her mind.

The next morning Spirit refused to eat more than a few handfuls of his feed, even though Ellie stood beside him trying to tempt him. She was worried because she had found a soft swelling under his tummy. It was filled with fluid and, although it didn't seem to hurt him when she touched it, it made up her mind. She found her uncle and asked if he could call the vet. He still seemed in a bad mood with her about the night before, but she suspected Ray had spoken to him about Spirit because he agreed to phone the surgery. John, the vet, arranged to come later that afternoon when Ellie was back from school.

Ellie stared unseeingly at her school books that day as she tried not to think about something being really wrong with Spirit.

She was first in line at the bus stop when school finished. The bus seemed to take ages as it chugged from stop to stop. Ellie fidgeted in her seat, just wanting to get back.

Luke was waiting to pick her up – on his own this time. She ran to the car and got in. 'Hi.'

'Hi, there,' he greeted her and started the engine. 'I hear John's coming to see Spirit this afternoon?'

Ellie nodded.

'So he's still not eating?'

'No,' said Ellie, chewing a nail.

Luke gave her a reassuring smile. 'He'll be OK. Spirit's tough.'

Ellie hugged her bag to her chest, hoping he was right.

When they reached the stables, Ellie didn't even bother changing but ran straight to Spirit's stall. The door was slightly open. Was it the vet? She hadn't seen his car.

But reaching it, she saw that it was just Joe. He was rubbing Spirit's ears, murmuring to him. 'Hi,' he said, looking round.

'Hi.' Ellie dumped her school bag by the door and went to Spirit. 'How come you're here?'

Joe shrugged. 'I just thought I'd come and see him.'

Ellie frowned. There was something strange about Joe's voice. A tightness. She could feel a tension coming from him.

'How's he been today?' she asked.

'Not really himself,' Joe admitted. 'I tried turning him out, but he just stood by the gate so I brought him in again. I've just been doing some T-Touch circles on his ears. They're supposed to be good for horses when they're ill.'

'He seems to like it.' Ellie looked at Spirit's half-shut eyes and lowered head. It was so unlike him to stand still and let someone else stroke him, but she could feel a contentment coming from him as Joe smoothed his mane. 'John'll be here soon. He'll find out what the matter is. I guess it must be a virus or –'

'Ellie . . .' Joe cut across her. She looked at him. Now there was no mistaking it: his face was tense, his expression worried.

'What?' she said when he didn't speak again.

'It might not be just a virus.'

'What do you mean? What are you talking about?'

Joe pushed a hand through his hair. 'I looked up Spirit's symptoms on the Internet – being listless, off his feed, the lumps, the swelling on his belly . . .'

'And?' Ellie's voice rose in alarm. Spirit's eyes blinked open, his head lifting. She put a hand on his face. 'What did you find?'

'It could be something called lymphosarcoma. It's a cancer.'

The word fell into the air between them. A million thoughts swirled through Ellie's head, but all she could do was echo Joe. '*Cancer?*'

'It may not be,' Joe said quickly. 'It's really rare in horses. But I just thought you'd better know.'

Ellie looked at Spirit, shaking her head. 'It's not cancer.' Lifting his face to hers, Spirit breathed out softly. *No. It isn't cancer. It couldn't be. I won't let it be.*

'Ellie!' Luke called from outside. 'John's just arrived!'

Joe went to the door. 'She's in here.'

Ellie heard John's footsteps. As he appeared in the stable doorway, Spirit snorted and stepped back, his eyes wary.

'It's OK,' Ellie soothed him.

'So what's up then?' John's eyes were taking in the untouched feed in the manger and the way Spirit's ribs were showing. 'Is he off his food?'

'Yes, and he's coughing sometimes. He's got some

lumps too.' Ellie glanced at Joe who was watching from the door. He gave her an encouraging look. She was glad he was there. Even though he had spoken her worst fears out loud, he was her best friend and she knew how much he cared.

John let Spirit sniff him, then he walked around, checking him over. Spirit kept his head high. Ellie could tell he was anxious having the vet around him, but he stayed still as she stroked him and murmured softly.

John took out his thermometer. He took Spirit's temperature and then put on his stethoscope and listened to Spirit's chest. Ellie saw him frown slightly as his fingers felt the small bumps under Spirit's skin. He then moved to Spirit's head and checked under his chin and jaw, and finally felt the soft swelling on Spirit's stomach. His expression became more serious.

'What's the matter with him?' Ellie asked.

'Hard to say for sure.' John rubbed his chin. 'His temperature is pretty much OK, but his heart rate's high. I'll take a blood test. With the signs he's showing – being off his food, being listless – it could be any one of a number of things. I don't like the look of this ventral oedema though – the swelling here – and these lumps. They may be nothing, but I want to take a biopsy of one just in case. I'll send that off to the lab.' He set to work, getting needles out. Spirit flinched, but stood still as John collected blood for testing and a sample of one of the lumps on his chest.

Finally, John put everything away in his bag and then stroked Spirit for a few moments, as if trying to make up his mind what to say.

'Look, you're a sensible lass,' he said, turning to Ellie at last. 'It's maybe just a virus, but I need to tell you, we could be looking at something worse.'

For a moment, Ellie wanted to simply turn and run. She swallowed and stroked Spirit. 'What . . . what do you mean?'

'There's a rare form of cancer in horses called lymphosarcoma – it's not common at all, I've only ever seen three cases in my life, but when it does strike, it's not good news.'

Ellie looked at Spirit's beautiful face, his long forelock falling over his dark eyes. She had to swallow hard to speak. 'Do . . . do they die from it?'

John sighed. 'Yes. And they go fast. There's very little you can do with lympho. The cancer forms in the lymph nodes and spreads around the body into the different organs. By the time the horse is showing signs, it's too late to do anything about it. If it has spread, then you're really only looking at the horse having a month or so to live.'

Joe came forward from the door, his face full of concern. 'He hasn't definitely got lymphosarcoma though, has he, John? It could still be just a virus.'

John nodded. 'The tests may show up something else completely. You just need to be prepared.'

Ellie nodded, unable to speak.

'How long will the tests take to come back?' Joe asked for her.

'Only a day or two for the bloods, about five days for the biopsy – we'll have to send the sample off to the lab. I'll ring when I hear anything.' John went to the door.

'Thank you,' Ellie whispered.

John left the stable. Ellie found she couldn't move.

'Ellie?' Joe said quietly.

A sob burst from her.

'Oh, Ellie.' She turned blindly into him. Joe's arms tightened around her. Behind, she heard Spirit snort in confusion, but she was incapable of turning to him, incapable of doing anything but crying as all the fears that she'd been trying to ignore over the last week finally rose up and overwhelmed her. All she had lost in the last ten months filled her head – her mum, her dad, her old life in New Zealand. She couldn't lose Spirit as well.

Joe stroked her back. She rested her head against his chest, slowly regaining control, feeling his damp T-shirt under her cheek.

'It'll be OK,' he whispered. 'It will. You know it will.'

Ellie forced herself to believe him. It would be OK. Luke's words from earlier echoed through her head:

Spirit's tough. He was right. Spirit had been through so much. He would be fine.

There was a shout from the yard. 'I'll tell the others and keep them away for the moment,' Joe said. 'You stay here.'

'Thanks.' More than anything right then, Ellie wanted to talk properly to Spirit, to hear his voice.

Joe left and she rested her head against Spirit's forehead, shutting her eyes and reaching out to him with her thoughts. *Spirit?*

The energy change was swift. She felt their thoughts merge.

I'm here.

Ellie stroked his neck, her eyes closed still. *You're sick, maybe really sick.*

Yes.

His simple acceptance brought the tears to her eyes again. *Why didn't you say?*

Because there is nothing you can do.

Spirit!

He didn't say anything else. She probed deeper into his feelings, looking for anxiety, worry, panic. But instead all she found was a feeling of deep calm.

Aren't you scared? she asked.

No. She could feel his surprise now.

But . . . She could hardly bring herself to think it, but she had to. *But you might have cancer – you might die.*

As she voiced the thought, she felt sick.

I'm here now. We must walk in the present. The simplicity of his thought was clear. She opened her eyes. All that mattered to him was that he was here now and so was she. She hugged him, not knowing quite what to say, comforted by his calm, but also with a million questions and fears buzzing round in her head.

If you are really sick, I'll help you, she promised him. *I'll do everything I can.*

I know. You always do. He nuzzled her and Ellie's heart clenched painfully as she saw the absolute trust in his eyes.

Chapter Six

When Ellie left the stable, she felt calmer, determined. She went into the house to change out of her school clothes. Her uncle was sitting at the kitchen table talking to Luke and Joe. He broke off as she came in. 'John's told me about that grey of yours,' he grunted.

Ellie didn't want to talk about it – least of all with her uncle. She saw Joe and Luke both give her a look of sympathy.

'So, the tests will be back in a few days then?'

She nodded.

'You'll decide what to do then.'

'Decide?' Ellie realized what her uncle meant. 'You mean decide whether to put him to sleep or not?' Her voice rose.

Len huffed out a breath. 'Well, you're not going to keep a dying horse, are you?'

'Dad!' Joe protested.

Len looked surprised. 'What?'

'Don't say things like that. Spirit might not have cancer anyway.'

Len pointed at Ellie. 'There's no point pussy-footing round this. If that horse of hers isn't going to get better, then he's going to have to be shot.'

'Spirit's isn't going to be shot!' Ellie struggled to control her anger.

'It'll be the only thing for it. Put him out of his misery. The sooner, the better.'

Ellie's temper snapped. 'What? Just give up on him? Like you did on Merlin, you mean? No. Even if Spirit has cancer I'm not having him shot. I'm not like you!'

Len pushed his chair back, his face darkening. 'I won't be spoken to like that.'

'Well, then don't talk about Spirit,' Ellie shouted. 'You've got no say in what happens to him. No say at all so keep out of it!'

'That's enough! Be quiet!' Len roared.

'Or what?' Ellie retorted furiously. 'You'll hit me like you'd hit Joe?'

Ellie heard Joe's intake of breath and was aware of Luke leaping to his feet.

Len's fists clenched but Luke was suddenly in front of her. 'Len! She's a fourteen-year-old girl and she's upset. Don't be stupid!'

Len and Luke stared at each other, the air bristling

between them. Ellie was reminded of the moment of stillness before two dogs fight.

A sob burst out of her. The sound punctured the tension and both Len and Luke seemed to breathe out. Luke took a half-step back so he was beside Ellie, his eyes still on Len. Len watched him for a moment, his fists relaxing. Ellie could see the rage fading from his face, sense returning to him.

As if in mutual agreement, they both turned away. Ellie just wanted to get out of there. She could feel hot tears at the back of her eyes and she didn't want to cry in front of her uncle. She swung round and ran through the door to the hall.

'Ellie!' she heard Joe's voice.

'Don't you dare go after her!' Len ground out.

Ellie wondered for a moment if Joe would defy Len, but he didn't. She ran up the stairs and didn't hear any more. Reaching her bedroom, she shut the door and sank down against it, her face in her hands as she gave way to the tears.

'I'm sorry to hear about Spirit.' Helen came over to her with Sasha when Ellie eventually returned to the yard, her face washed but her eyes still red. 'Joe told us what John said.'

'Yeah,' Sasha added. 'Hopefully, the tests will come back OK and it'll just be something minor, Ellie.'

'Thanks.' The two grooms' concern for Spirit

made her uncle's lack of sympathy stand out even more. Even Sasha looked genuinely worried for her.

'You've got Gem and Picasso to ride tonight, haven't you?' said Helen. 'We've groomed them for you. You just need their tack.'

Ellie smiled gratefully. 'Thanks.'

She went to fetch Picasso's saddle and bridle. Luke was in the tackroom, taking a saddle off a rack. She stopped awkwardly when she saw him, remembering the scene in the kitchen.

'How are you doing?' he asked her.

'OK,' she answered automatically, then swallowed. 'Well, you know.'

He nodded. 'I hope Spirit's OK.'

'Thanks. And thanks for earlier. I kind of lost it.' Ellie sighed.

'Anyone would. Len can be a real . . .' Luke broke off. 'Just don't make a habit of yelling at him like that – at least if I'm not there.'

As she looked into his eyes, she felt suddenly comforted. 'I won't have Spirit shot.'

'Let's just hope he's all right, that the tests show something that can be cured.' Luke smiled. 'I'd put money on the fact that if anything can be done to help him, you'll do it.'

Ellie thought the days before hearing the test results would never pass. Everyone on the yard, apart from her uncle, was supportive. Even Sasha helped her with her other chores so Ellie would have more time with Spirit. Sasha had already started seeing a new boyfriend, and from what Ellie overheard her saying to Helen, she really liked him. So, although Sasha was still cool with Luke, she wasn't too angry or upset.

Ellie spent every second she could with Spirit, grooming him, hand-feeding him, leading him out down the lane to graze on the bank of lush grass there. She was up early every morning and often stayed out in the stables until ten o'clock, only coming in when the light finally faded. Even the arrival of the mare Fern and her three-week-old foal on the yard didn't distract her.

Fern was the mare Len had sold to his friend Bob. Now Bob's horses were all being sold off, Len had bought her back at half the price and so was very pleased with his deal.

'What's the foal called?' Ellie asked Joe as they walked past the mare and foal's paddock on the day they arrived.

'Her show name's Oakmist Fantasia. She doesn't have a stable name yet. We'll have to think of one. Dad will probably just call her "the foal" for now.'

Ellie watched the foal trotting round in circles. She was gorgeous. She had a fluffy chestnut coat and a sticking-up, cream-coloured mane and short tail. Her legs were long and gangly like Bambi's, her dark eyes large. Seeing Ellie and Joe, the foal halted and stared at them, her tiny ears pricked, her expression full of intelligence.

As Ellie looked at her face, a prickle ran over her skin. For a moment, she felt drawn to the foal, almost like she had to Spirit when she had first met him. The filly's eyes met Ellie's, but then she tossed her head and wheeled away, kicking up her heels almost defiantly.

'She's gorgeous, isn't she?' Joe said.

'Yeah.' Ellie frowned and then shook her head, dismissing the feelings. Of course she wanted to look at the foal – all foals were cute and this one was particularly pretty.

'Look at her fan club,' Joe said, nodding to where the geldings were watching from the fence. They were all staring adoringly at the filly. Gem in particular looked besotted. He was hanging his head over the top rail, his eyes goofy as he watched the little foal who was now showing off, prancing around in front of him.

'She's going to be a character,' Joe said. 'When she came out of the horsebox, she was really wary of everyone. She wouldn't leave Fern's side and she even tried to kick Stuart, but since she's been out in the field she's started relaxing. Mind you, she still doesn't want to come near any human. I don't think she's been handled much at all.'

'The journey must have been really upsetting for her as well,' Ellie said, thinking how it must have seemed through the filly's eyes. She wouldn't have known where she was going or what was happening. If the only contact she'd had with humans since she'd been born was being forced into a horsebox, it was no wonder she was feeling wary of people.

Joe nodded. 'Hopefully, she'll settle down soon. Fern's lovely. She's won loads of lightweight working hunter classes. She could have been a show jumper, I reckon. Dad's really pleased to have her back and to have her foal. She should make a really good brood mare if this filly's anything to go by.'

Ellie glanced again at the foal, but then she remembered Spirit. How was he? She caught him and brought him in from the field. Once he was in his stable she checked him over, her heart sinking. He still had the lumps on his chest; they seemed bigger and the swelling on his tummy had grown too.

The next morning, she had a phone call from John before she went to school. The results of the blood tests were back. They showed anaemia and a high white blood cell count, which John said didn't look good but still didn't prove anything definite. They had to wait for the biopsy results, which would not be through until Monday.

It was a long weekend for Ellie. She had to help her uncle at a show on Sunday, although none of the ponies she rode were competing. She wanted to stay with Spirit, but there was no way she would be allowed to miss it. Thankfully, there was so much to do she didn't have time to think about Spirit much. Joe was riding Wisp and his working hunter pony, Barney, and two of the livery horses were also going: Darcey and Willow who were owned by clients of Len. Ellie hoped she and Joe would be able to sit and talk in the horsebox on the way there – she'd been so busy with Spirit she hadn't seen much of Joe all week, but Len made Joe sit in the cab with him.

Ellie noticed more and more as the day went on that Len was keeping them apart, or making sure he was around if they were together.

The only time he left them alone was when Ray arrived at the show and Len went for a drink with him mid-afternoon after most of the classes his ponies were entered in had finished. Joe and Ellie sat on the ramp of the box, chatting. It was just great to be together. Len came back, looking like he was in a good mood.

'I want a word with you, Joe.'

'Sure,' Joe said, looking at him expectantly.

'On your own.'

Ellie shrugged. 'I'll go and check what class is on.' There was just the Intermediate Championship that

Joe had qualified Wisp for still to go. She left them to it.

When she returned, Joe was preparing Wisp for the championship while Len sorted some things out in the living accommodation. 'So what did your dad want to talk to you about?' Ellie asked curiously.

'Nothing,' Joe muttered.

'Nothing?'

'Well, something.' Joe shook his head. 'We can talk about it later.' Ellie saw that he looked really unhappy.

'Are you OK?' she asked in concern.

'I really can't talk about it now. The championship will be starting soon. Can you finish Wisp off while I change?'

'Sure.' Ellie frowned and watched him go into the living accommodation. What was going on? What had Len said to him? He'd been fine before.

She got Wisp ready, repainting his hooves, tightening his girth and running a cloth over his sleek sandy coat, still puzzling about it.

Joe seemed distracted throughout the championship and Wisp played up, cantering on the wrong leg and tossing his head. He wasn't chosen as champion or reserve. However, to Ellie's astonishment, Len seemed fairly philosophical. 'Never mind. Another time,' he said as Joe came out.

Joe nodded and dismounted.

'Guess you had a bit on your mind, lad.' Len nodded at Ellie. 'So, have you told her then?'

'No.'

'Told me what?' Ellie demanded.

Len met her gaze. 'Joe's going to Canada.'

'Canada?' Ellie stared in surprise. 'For a holiday?'

Len folded his arms, satisfaction clear on his face. 'No, to live.' He took in her astonishment. 'He's going to work for Ray for a year, aren't you, lad?'

Joe gave a brief nod, his eyes on Ellie. He looked desperate.

Ellie's head spun. No. Joe couldn't go. She needed him, particularly now. 'When?' she whispered.

'Three weeks, just as soon as his exams finish,' pronounced Len.

Ellie felt as if the ground had abruptly vanished from under her feet.

'Right, let's take this pony back to the lorry,' Len said, starting to lead Wisp away.

'I'm just getting a drink from the cafe,' said Joe, shooting a look at Ellie.

'Me too,' she said quickly.

And before Len could stop them, they had set off across the show ground together. 'Oi! Come back here!' he shouted, but they quickly lost themselves in the crowd.

As soon as they were safely away, Ellie grabbed Joe's arm. 'You can't go!'

'I don't want to, Ellie,' he protested. 'But Dad's sorted it all out with Ray today.'

'Well, make him unsort it. Tell him you won't leave.'

'I tried. I even asked if I could wait a bit, maybe go next year or after the summer – I don't want to leave while Spirit's so ill – but he says I have to go as soon as possible.'

'Why?'

A blush spread across Joe's cheekbones. 'Because . . . because of you.'

'Me?'

'Well, us. He thinks there's something going on and, you know, with us being cousins and stuff it's freaking him out.'

Ellie hit her head with her hands. 'But there isn't anything happening!'

'He won't believe it. I tried to tell him, but you know what Dad's like – he gets a bee in his bonnet about something and he just won't listen. He's convinced of it.'

Ellie stared at him. 'Well, we'll make him believe it. He can't just send you away. You can't go.'

Joe looked at her helplessly. 'I have to. He's made up his mind.'

'So?' Ellie exclaimed. 'Fight him! Refuse to go!'

'I can't!' Joe's voice rose.

'You can! Please!' Tears sprang to her eyes. 'I need you to stay here.'

She saw the conflict written across his face and suddenly she knew there was nothing she could say to change things. She could see it in his eyes. He wasn't going to fight. Her anger was replaced by a feeling of deep despair. She couldn't imagine not having Joe to talk to and hang round with.

'I'll email. Phone. And I'll be back in a year's time. It's not forever.'

Ellie swallowed. 'Yeah. Whatever.' She looked away, hoping he wouldn't see the tears in her eyes. 'We should buy that drink.'

'Don't be mad at me,' he beseeched.

'Well, don't go then!' Wrapping her arms tightly across her chest, she marched to the cafe. Joe sighed and followed her without saying another word.

Ellie was glad she was by herself in the horsebox on the way home. She needed time to think. Although she couldn't bear the thought of Joe leaving, through her despair there was another little voice filtering in. Joe would have an amazing time in Canada, she was sure. He certainly needed to be away from his dad. He wouldn't be bullied any more, shouted at, put down. Ray would teach him so much. He'd always wanted to work on a yard where they used natural horsemanship techniques. *It's a good thing for him*, she told herself.

But what about me?

Taking a deep breath, she reminded herself of all the times Joe had helped her and been there for her since she'd arrived at High Peak Stables and she pushed down her anger and misery. She mustn't be mad with him and make him feel awful. As they left the motorway and headed up into the mountains, Ellie came to a decision. Even though part of her felt hurt and betrayed that Joe wouldn't fight it, she was going to try and be unselfish. It was going to happen whether she liked it or not and seeing as Joe was her best friend, she would try to be supportive however hard it was.

Swallowing, she rested her head against the window of the horsebox. It was beginning to feel like she was trapped in a nightmare. Joe was leaving and, she realized with a shiver, the results of Spirit's biopsy were due the next day.

She stared out of the window, her stomach tying itself in knots, as they chugged on through the dark night.

Chapter Seven

The phone call Ellie had been dreading came after school. Even across the phone line she could hear the serious note in John's deep voice. 'Ellie, it's not good news.'

Five minutes later, Ellie walked down the yard, everything feeling as if it was distorted, removed from reality. Turning towards Spirit's stable, she broke into a run. He was standing, one hind leg resting, his neck low but as she opened the door he lifted his head and whinnied.

The words John had just spoken to her echoed through her head. '*It* is *lymphosarcoma . . . It's spread through his body and is untreatable . . . He'll gradually lose more and more weight . . . He won't have long . . . At some point you will have to make the decision to have him put to sleep . . .*'

'No!' Ellie burst out with a sob.

Spirit breathed on her face in surprise.

She felt as if she was falling, plummeting through

the air with no safety net or anything to catch her. He was going to die. She cried and cried, while Spirit nuzzled her patiently.

At last the tears dried up, and in the peace and quiet Ellie felt their minds merge.

Oh, Spirit. She didn't know what to say. How could she explain?

She didn't have to.

I think I am going to die.

No! Ellie couldn't bear it.

I am.

How do you know? she asked him.

I can feel it. Deep inside. My energy's fading. I'm getting weaker.

Ellie shook her head. *You're ill, but we can do stuff. There're all sorts of things we can try.*

I am not afraid of dying.

But I'm *afraid of you dying!*

She felt the change in his feelings. He raised his head and looked at her. 'I am,' she whispered out loud, stroking his cheek. 'Please . . . don't die. I need you, Spirit.'

He breathed out softly. *Then I will stay.*

When Ellie finally left the stable, Joe was the first person she saw. He took one look at her face and knew. 'So you've spoken to John?'

She nodded, her throat too tight to talk.

'Oh, Els.' Joe came over and took her hands. 'I'm so sorry.'

He moved to put his arms round her but, shaking her head, Ellie pulled away. She didn't want to cry any more just then; she didn't want to be comforted. She wanted to change things – make it all better.

'I'm going inside,' she managed to say. 'To look on the Internet.'

'OK. Do you want me to tell everyone?'

She nodded and then went to the computer. She found out all she could about lymphosarcoma. Time and time again she read words that all said the same: *most cases do not survive more than a week or a few months.*

She rubbed her eyes. She couldn't accept it – she wouldn't. There *had* to be something she could do. John had ruled out chemotherapy or aggressive drugs on the phone. He believed the cancer had spread too far through Spirit's body. Ellie followed links to holistic sites that suggested a number of different therapies and remedies. She made a list of everything: herbal extracts, Bach flower remedies, Chinese medicine, acupuncture. Her grandmother in New Zealand kept her supplied with a generous allowance and most of the time Ellie had nothing to spend it on because her life revolved around the horses. She would use all the money she had to buy whatever remedies were supposed to help. She would do whatever it took. She *would* make him better.

Over the next few weeks, Ellie tried everything. Ignoring her uncle's mockery, she ordered flower remedies and herbs and fed them to Spirit on apples and carrots which he ate, she sensed, more to please her than because he wanted to. She hand-fed him mashes flavoured with fresh mint or molasses and honey. She massaged him with healing aroma-therapy oils and even called in an acupuncturist. Her gran was lovely, promising to give her all the money she needed.

Ellie tried healing him herself. When she'd been little, she'd had the feeling that she could sense pain in animals' bodies and, by putting her hands where the pain was, she could help ease it. She wasn't sure if it ever worked and actually did any good, but she'd always hoped it had. She remembered it now. If she could talk to horses, maybe it wasn't so mad to think she could heal them too. Since she had met Ray she had been reading on the Internet about people who could communicate with animals. Many of them also talked about being able to heal too so she tried placing her hands on him and letting energy flow through her, listening to her instincts and letting her hands move around his body just as they said they did.

When she touched him and let her hands be guided by her instincts, feeling her fingertips pulsing and tingling as she moved them gently over his body, his eyes would half close and his head sink down. He would often sway slightly as he relaxed and sigh. She wasn't sure it helped him though.

I like it, he told her one night when she asked. He was lying down and she was curled up beside him. *It does help. Everything you have been doing helps.*

But I don't just want to help. I want to make you well again, she told him. *Are you getting better?*

He breathed softly on her hands. *No.*

Ellie bit her lip. *What can I do? How can I heal you?*

He sent her a wave of comfort. *Some things can't be healed. Some battles can't be won.*

But Ellie refused to accept that. *This one can, Spirit! It can. I'm not going to give up. I'm going to make you better.*

He simply looked at her, his dark eyes wise.

Ellie refused to be put off. Even though she could feel the weariness inside him, she could tell that he was happy in his life. She knew he liked being with her in the stable or walking down the lane. And he was content when he was out in the field, nuzzling the other horses, enjoying their company, or standing watching the little filly who was still just called 'the foal'.

With her thoughts so full of Spirit, Ellie was able to almost forget about Joe going to Canada. But the three weeks passed, his exams came and went, and suddenly, almost before she knew it, it was the night before he was due to leave. Hardly able to believe it, Ellie went into his room. His suitcase was packed, his electric guitar was in its case and he was just putting the last few things into a rucksack. He smiled at her and she sat down on his bed. His room looked strange – his desk was clear and on his bookcase there were patches in the dust where there had been photos, books and CDs.

'You're really going,' she said.

He nodded. 'I am. Just think – tomorrow I'll be in Canada.'

Ellie saw the conflict in his eyes. She knew he hated leaving her, but she could sense the excitement in him too. She felt torn between feeling happy for him and yet not wanting him to go. 'You'd better email lots.'

'Just try and stop me.' Joe fastened up the top of his rucksack and then looked at her. 'I'll miss you.'

She didn't know how she would manage without him, but she let the better part of herself triumph and with a tremendous effort forced a smile, making herself be strong for him. 'I'll miss you too, but I'll be OK. You'll have a brilliant time in Canada and while you're there you can tell me about everything you're learning.'

Their gazes met and for a moment they just looked at each other.

Joe sighed. 'Come on. Come with me while I say goodbye to the horses.'

They went out on to the quiet dark yard. Joe worked his way round all the stables, saying a goodbye to each horse. He paused at an empty stable in the pony barn. It was cleaned out and bare of rugs, deserted. Ellie saw Joe swallow and knew he was thinking about Merlin. He went to the door and looked inside. Ellie swallowed. She could picture the merry little bay pony, too small to look properly over the door. He had been the first pony she'd ridden when she had come to High Peak Stables. She went to Joe and put her arm over his shoulder. 'He was the best pony,' she said softly.

Joe glanced at her, his eyes infinitely sad. 'He was.'

'Your dad should never have had him put to sleep.'

'No.' Joe shut his eyes. 'Ellie, I don't want to leave you, but I'm glad I'm going. I want to get away from here.'

Ellie nodded, understanding.

They stared at the empty stable for a few moments, each deep in their own thoughts, while around them the ponies snorted and pulled at their haynets in the warm summer night.

Chapter Eight

Joe left early the next morning. 'You have to keep trying with Spirit,' he told Ellie as he hugged her before he left. 'There's going to be something that will work. I know there is and you'll find it.'

Ellie hugged him and then waved him off with the others.

'I can't believe he's gone,' she said to Luke.

Luke shook his head as the car drove away and the grooms walked back to the yard. 'He should have told Len he wouldn't go until the end of the summer. I can't get over him leaving when –' He broke off. 'Well, when there's so much happening. He shouldn't have gone.'

'He wanted to stay.' Ellie struggled to come to Joe's defence. 'He really did. He asked if he could but he wasn't allowed to.'

Luke looked at her, his mouth set. 'No one could have forced him on that plane if he'd refused.'

Ellie turned away. Right then, she had enough to

think about with Spirit without wasting energy on wishing that Joe was made differently. He'd gone. She had to deal with it.

'So, what are you going to do about Spirit?' Luke asked, falling into step beside her.

'Do?' She shrugged. 'Nothing. Just keep trying – keep fighting.'

Luke nodded. For a moment, she thought he was about to say something else, but then he just gave her a smile. 'Good luck with it.'

'Thanks,' Ellie sighed.

By the following weekend Spirit had completely stopped eating, his ribs were standing out more sharply than ever and he had become very quiet. When Ellie turned him out in the field on Saturday, he didn't graze with the others but stayed near the gate. Resting a back foot, he half-closed his eyes and lowered his head. Ellie waited, expecting to see the other horses going over to him, but they stayed away.

'See you later,' she called anxiously to him. He raised his head but couldn't even summon the energy to whinny.

He barely moved all day. At suppertime Ellie went to bring him in while Luke caught Gem and Picasso. Len and Stuart were driving down to Cornwall with some of the Armstrongs' ponies. They were staying overnight there and going in a show the next day.

Ellie looked at Spirit. Deep inside her she felt a knot of fear but she tried to ignore it. She called his name. His ears flickered but he didn't open his eyes. She called again. 'Spirit!'

This time he did raise his head. Her heart clenched – his eyes were duller now and she could feel the pain radiating from him.

'Hey, boy.' She put on his headcollar, her voice falsely cheerful. 'Time to go in.'

Luke had already reached the gate with Gem and Picasso. 'Ellie, he's not looking good,' he said in concern as Ellie walked Spirit over.

'He's OK,' Ellie said stubbornly.

She led Spirit slowly to his stable. He stumbled every few strides. She had put down a fresh bed for him that day and filled a haynet in the hope that he would eat, but he didn't take even a mouthful. She stroked him. His skin felt tight and she could feel her fingertips tingling with heat as she passed them over his body, feeling his energy adjusting slightly. The lumps on his chest had grown bigger and she'd noticed that he had some sores on his flanks now.

Ellie left the stable and went to do the feeds with Luke before they shut the barns and the tackroom up. For once, Luke was quiet as they worked. As they finished, he turned to Ellie. 'So, have you talked to John about when you should have Spirit put down?'

Ellie's heart lurched. John *had* spoken to her about it and he had said the decision was hers. When she felt it was time she should give him a ring. Ellie was determined not to make that call, though. She wouldn't give up on Spirit. Not ever. She looked away, not answering.

Luke's face was serious. 'At some point you'll have to make the decision.'

'No! He's going to get better.'

'Ellie,' Luke said softly. 'He's not going to get better now. You can't let him suffer any longer. It's incredible that he's still here. He hasn't eaten for days. He's surviving on will power alone and you have to do what's best for him.'

'Killing him is best for him?' A desperate part of her still fought to avoid the truth.

'Yes.'

Ellie swung round to march out, not wanting to hear any more, but Luke grabbed her arm, stopping her escape. 'I know it hurts. But someone has to tell you – for your sake, for his. Given the state Spirit is in, it *is* best now to put him to sleep.'

Ellie wrenched her arm away. 'He's fine!' she spat.

Luke's voice raised. 'He's not fine, Ellie! Use your eyes!' He took a breath and lowered his tone. 'Please – you know I am no more likely to give up than you are, but there are some things you can't fight and sometimes giving up is the right thing to do. Put

Spirit first. Don't let him starve to death. Let him die peacefully.'

'He wants to stay.' Ellie's voice trembled, tears welling. 'He doesn't want to go.'

Luke didn't say anything.

'He doesn't, Luke!'

With a shake of his head, Luke walked away.

Ellie ran to Spirit's stable. He was lying down and he lifted his head to look at her as she opened his door, but Ellie could see the effort he had to make. She walked over and sat down beside him without speaking. Outside the scent of honeysuckle was heavy in the evening air. It seemed so unfair that summer was in full force, flowers blooming and plants growing, while Spirit's life was ebbing away in front of her eyes.

Because that was what was happening – Luke was right. She had to be brave and face it. Her shoulders sagged as the fight finally went out of her.

Sitting down beside him, she stroked his face. She let herself see that there were deep hollows above his eyes now, pain tightening his muzzle and lips. She remembered what Luke had just said: *It's incredible he's still alive . . .*

It *was* incredible. She knew deep down that the only thing keeping him there was his amazing will – the promise he had made to her. *I will stay.*

Ellie felt a lump in her throat. She shut her eyes

and felt the connection slowly open between them.

His voice in her head was weary. *It hurts. I'm so tired.*

Every bit of Ellie fought against the question she knew she had to ask. *Do you want to go?*

She held her breath. There was a moment's silence and then Spirit spoke. *No, I said I will stay.*

Spirit . . . She swallowed. If she really loved him she would let him go peacefully and before he was in any more pain. She couldn't ask him to battle on like this. *It's all right. You've tried so hard. You don't have to try any longer. The vet can give you an injection and you'll go to sleep. It'll take away the pain. You . . . you won't ever wake up but the pain will be gone.*

Her fingers trembled as they played with his mane.

Death. There was no fear, only acceptance.

Her heart ached. *Yes.*

Neither of them spoke. Ellie put her arms round him, feeling as if she was splintering into millions of pieces that were floating up into the sky. He snorted, sending her waves of comfort despite his own pain and weariness. She started to sob. She didn't think she could bear it. But she had to. She couldn't let Spirit keep suffering just so she could keep him with her.

When? The question filled her brain.

She looked at the dullness in Spirit's eyes and knew

deep down it wouldn't be any easier if she put it off by a week or two, and it would be harder for him. *Tomorrow,* she thought. *I'll phone John tomorrow.*

She saw slight shivers crossing Spirit's skin despite the warm night. 'I'll bring you a rug,' she murmured.

She fetched a lightweight fleece rug. She didn't try to make Spirit get up so she could do it up; she just covered his body with it and then crept under it too, tucking herself between his front and back legs. She put her arm over his back. Spirit breathed slowly and deeply, his muzzle resting on the straw, his eyes half-closed. But Ellie felt too unhappy to sleep and stayed awake as the evening turned from dusk to darkness outside.

As she sat there, images ran through her mind – the first time she had seen Spirit at the sale, walking him back to the yard with Joe beside her when he had refused to load into the horsebox, the first time she had heard his voice and the first time she had sat on his back and ridden him. She thought about the sound of his joyful whinny in the mornings when he saw her walking to his stable, and the feel of his warm breath on her hair. She remembered how patient he'd been when she was learning to talk with other horses, how he had encouraged her and never blamed her when she got things wrong. *And all the time he helped me so much with other stuff too,* Ellie realized. If she hadn't been able to tell him about her parents and how much she missed them, she would have gone mad in her early months at High Peak Stables.

Looking at him, she felt her heart swell at how incredible he was. After the way he'd been treated by humans, after everything that had happened to him, he should have wanted nothing to do with people. But he hadn't let the experiences in his past destroy his ability to love and trust her. Now she had to repay that trust by being strong and giving him the one thing she could – freedom from pain. No matter how much it cost her, no matter how much it hurt, in the morning she would phone the vet.

Oh, Spirit, Spirit, Spirit, she thought.

There was a noise at the stable door and she glanced round to see Luke there. Her heart sank; she didn't want to speak to him.

'Are you all right?' he asked in a low voice.

She nodded.

'Do you want anything?'

She shook her head, her throat aching with tears.

Luke melted away into the night. Ellie rested her head against Spirit's neck and watched as the stars outside the stable changed in the sky and the hours slowly passed.

She finally drifted off to sleep. She woke to the sound of birds singing. Outside the stable, she could see the stars had faded and the grey light of morning was starting to lighten the sky. Spirit was stirring slightly. She stroked his neck, feeling her own leg muscles protesting at having been curled up all night. It was almost a new day. Soon, the house door would open and Luke would come out, then the grooms would arrive and then . . . then she would have to ring John.

She paused, expecting to feel the crashing weight of grief she had felt the night before, but it didn't come. She felt numb, like a steel barrier had gone up in her brain, separating her feelings from her thoughts.

She lay there until her watch said six thirty and then, with a feeling of unreal calmness settling over her, she stood up. Spirit put his front legs out and struggled to his feet too.

Maybe this will be the last time I'll ever see him stand up in his stable again after lying down . . .

No. She slammed the thought away. She gave him a kiss. 'I'll be back soon.'

Leaving the stable, she went to the house. Luke was in the kitchen, putting the kettle on. She wondered if he would ask why she had stayed in the stable, but he didn't. 'Coffee?'

'Yes, please. I'm just going to take a shower.'

When she came down, Luke had gone outside. There was a cup of coffee and a plate of toast waiting for her. Ellie bit off a mouthful, but she couldn't swallow it and ended up throwing the rest away.

She joined Luke in the feedroom. 'So?' he said, as she started to mechanically put out the buckets.

'I'm going to ring John this morning.'

Luke nodded. 'It's the right thing.'

Ellie could tell he was looking at her but she concentrated on the feeds. Luke didn't ask any more but as he passed by, he squeezed her arm.

At eight o'clock, Ellie went to the office and rang John at the surgery.

'It's time,' she managed to say. 'Can you come today?'

To her relief, she didn't need to explain. 'Of course,' he said. 'I'll come over about ten.'

'Can you . . . can you not shoot him but use an injection?' From being with her dad, Ellie knew that most vets preferred to shoot horses with a humane killer when they were putting them down. But she couldn't bear it. She knew she couldn't stand still and watch Spirit being shot. It was only a few months since she had watched John shoot Merlin. She knew she couldn't stand there and watch Spirit being shot too.

'All right,' said John. He sighed. 'You're doing the right thing, lass.'

Ellie swallowed, pain threatening to break through

the numbness for a moment. Why did everyone keep saying that she was doing the right thing when it certainly didn't feel right? It just felt so very, very wrong.

She put the phone down. Luke came to the doorway. 'Is John coming then?'

'Yes, at ten. Luke . . .' Ellie swallowed. There was something looming in her mind. She kept thinking about Merlin, about how the hunt kennels had come to take his body away to feed to the hounds. She still remembered hearing the huntsman driving the tractor and trailer across the field to collect him. 'Afterwards, when it's over . . .' She couldn't say it, but she saw the understanding dawn on Luke's face.

'Don't worry. I'll deal with that.'

'Not the hunt.'

'No. Not the hunt.' He looked at her. 'You go and see Spirit. Don't worry about that side of things.'

'Thanks.'

'Go on,' he said. 'Go.'

Ellie fetched Spirit's grooming kit and groomed him until his coat was sleek and his mane and tail hanging in silky strands. She oiled his hooves and cleaned his eyes and nose. It was as if by doing the normal things she could almost fool herself that what was about to happen wasn't real. He stood without being tied up, watching her all the time. Outside the stable,

Ellie heard the sound of a tractor. She vaguely wondered about it because usually only her uncle drove the tractor, but she quickly tuned out the noise to concentrate on Spirit.

As Ellie finished his face, she gazed at him, wanting to imprint him on her mind. She wanted to remember every single thing about him – the prick of his ears, the curve of his nostrils, the softness of the centre of his muzzle where she liked to kiss him. She wanted to fix it all forever in her mind.

Was this really going to be the last time she groomed him? She tried to imagine waking up the next morning without him being there, but it was impossible. It couldn't be. Life couldn't happen like that.

At ten o'clock, John appeared in the stable doorway with Luke. Ellie's heart seemed to miss a beat.

John gave her a compassionate look. 'Are you ready, lass?'

Ellie couldn't reply. She was fighting the urge to jump on Spirit's back and gallop him away, take him far, far away. Sensing her distress, Spirit nuzzled her.

Luke took charge. 'You'll need to bring him out into the empty field. John will do it there.'

Ellie put her hand on Spirit's neck and walked him to the door. She moved automatically, her feet feeling clumsy, her hands fumbling with his leadrope. The three of them and Spirit went out of the stable and into the fields. They walked up a slope to a quiet empty field. It backed on to the woods that covered the mountain around the stables.

'This seemed like a good spot,' said Luke. 'A private spot.' Ellie saw the mound of fresh brown earth lying on the lush grass halfway up the slope and realized Luke had dug a grave for Spirit. 'We can bury him here.'

Ellie was taken aback. She didn't know quite what she'd expected Luke to do with Spirit's body after John had put him to sleep, but she certainly hadn't imagined he would dig a grave. 'What will Uncle Len say?' she faltered.

'Leave that to me,' Luke told her. 'I'll deal with that when he gets back.'

Ellie looked round the field. It was the perfect place, with grey stone walls and trees around and a feeling of peace and quiet. In the blue sky above them a kestrel soared. Her eyes fell on the hole – Spirit's grave. For a moment, she felt the world spin.

Luke put his hand on her shoulder, anchoring her, grounding her.

'If you can get Spirit to stand alongside it, that would be grand,' said John.

Hardly aware of what she was doing, Ellie led Spirit over to the grave. He followed her trustingly, walking slowly. Only a month ago, he had been trotting and cantering around. Luke and John stood back for a few moments as she rested her forehead against Spirit's. She didn't care they were there; she opened her mind to his. *Spirit?*

Yes.

I love you.

She felt the waves of love come back from him, tinged with tiredness and pain but a love as certain as ever.

The barrier in her mind was cracking and anguish starting to flood through her as she felt reality closing in. This was really going to happen. They were going to put Spirit down. Every cell in her body wanted to hang on to him, to not let him go. Putting her arms round his neck, she felt his solid warmth. *I can't bear this, Spirit,* she thought desperately. *I just can't. It's too hard.*

Look for me. I'll be there.

Luke stepped forward. 'Ellie?'

John joined him. 'Are you ready?'

Ellie nodded dumbly, her heart breaking.

John opened his bag and got a syringe ready while Ellie stroked Spirit's face over and over again. He stood with his nose pressed against her. She could feel his absolute trust. After her parents had died, she had wished and wished that she could see them one more time just to say goodbye, but now she realized that being able to say goodbye didn't make parting any easier.

Stay with me, stay with me, stay with me, she pleaded to him in her head.

John placed his hand on Spirit's neck. 'Here we go.'

Almost before Ellie realized what was happening, John had started the injection, slowly releasing the deadly fluid into Spirit's veins – the drug that would stop his heart. She saw Spirit's ears flicker, felt his head start to sink. His eyes closed and he swayed slightly, his legs starting to buckle. John stood back. 'He might go down quick,' he warned.

As he spoke, Spirit's legs crumpled and he collapsed to the ground, falling on to his side. Ellie flung herself down beside him, cradling his head. *Spirit,* she thought over and over again.

Her horse, the horse who had taught her so much, who had loved her with his whole enormous heart . . .

She stroked his cheek, his nose, his forehead.

'Ellie, he's gone.' John's deep voice broke into her thoughts. She looked up at him. What did he mean? Spirit was still there. She looked down and saw that Spirit's ears were still, his eyes open and not blinking, his nostrils unmoving. Focusing now she felt the absolute absence of energy. He was dead.

No! In that moment, horror overwhelmed her. What had she done? She'd changed her mind. She wanted him back. It was too soon for him to go. She wasn't ready to be without him. She started to stroke him again. 'Spirit!' she begged. 'Come back!'

Luke crouched down beside her. 'It's over, Ellie.'

'No . . .' she started to shake her head. *'No!'*

Luke's arms pulled her close. She stared at him with shocked, wide eyes. He stroked her hair as John held the stethoscope to Spirit's chest, checking that his heart had stopped. The vet gave a brief nod and then Ellie felt herself start to shake – a dreadful, uncontrollable trembling as a tidal wave of grief engulfed her.

She couldn't bear it. 'Bring him back!' she sobbed into Luke's chest. 'I want him back!' It didn't feel long since she had been crying like this for her mum and dad. The old grief and the new mixed together, intense, overwhelming.

Luke held her tight and let her cry, his strong arms folded round her.

Chapter Nine

When Ellie's tears finally dried, Luke took her back to the house. John was already there, talking to Helen. They fell quiet as Ellie came in. She sat down silently at the table.

John glanced at Luke. 'Shall I give you a hand?'

With a cold shock, Ellie realized he meant with burying Spirit's body.

Luke looked at her. 'Do you want to be there?'

She shook her head. Spirit was gone. She didn't need to see him being buried.

'Thanks,' Luke said to John.

They left Ellie with Helen. 'Shall I make you a cup of tea?' Helen asked sympathetically.

'No, thanks. I'm . . . I'm going upstairs for a while.' Ellie spoke flatly, her voice sounding like a robot's.

'Sure. I'll be down here if you want me. I'm really sorry, Ellie. We all are.'

Ellie pulled off her boots and walked up the stairs.

Reaching her room, she lay down on the bed, curling her knees up to her chest, hugging herself into the tightest ball possible. She felt as though there was a great gaping hole in her, a hole that would never be filled again. Tears started to seep down her cheeks as she thought about Spirit, picturing him, imagining life without him. The pain battered through her.

She sobbed until her head hurt with crying. Afterwards, she lay there numbly, getting her breath back, noticing the quiet and stillness of the room. She began to think about Spirit again, remembering his whinny, knowing she would never hear it again, never feel his breath on her hands. Within minutes, fresh tears had started.

Eventually, Ellie exhausted herself and fell into a fitful sleep. She woke up when Luke came into her room to check on her. Sitting up, she stared at him in a daze.

Not bothering to ask if he could come in, he came over and sat down on the bed. 'I'm sorry you had to go through that. I'm sorry you had to feel it. I know how tough it is.'

Anger flared up inside her, fuelled by grief. She knew it was unfair, but she felt the overwhelming need to lash out at someone. 'You don't know! How can you?' she cried.

'I do know. Two of my ponies had to be put down.'

'Maggie?' said Ellie, remembering that Luke had once told her about his first pony, Maggie – how she had twisted a gut when she had colic.

'Yes. Then after Maggie I got Sparks and after Sparks, Bella. She was a show jumping pony, a total lunatic in the ring, but I loved her. We were doing really well together but one day the groom turned her out into a different field, one that our neighbour had rented out to us, and when I went to fetch her I found that she was trembling and having fits. She'd been poisoned.'

'How?' whispered Ellie, distracted for a moment from her own grief.

Luke's face was shadowed. 'It was just one of those fluke things that sometimes happen with horses. She'd found some cowbane and eaten it. The groom should have checked the field out, but he hadn't. Cowbane's deadly. Sometimes horses get better after a few days, but Bella didn't. She'd eaten too much of it; the fits got worse. She was in so much pain. Mum and Dad were away as usual and I had to make the decision to put her down.' He shook his head, lost in his memories. 'I could have kept her alive for a week longer but I had to do what was best for her.'

Ellie didn't speak. She realized there was so much she still didn't know about Luke.

Luke's eyes met hers. 'I know it won't feel like it now, but you made the right choice,' he said gently.

'You stopped him from having to suffer any more. Sometimes that's all we can do.'

Ellie turned away. It might have been the right choice, but knowing that didn't help the despair inside.

Luke squeezed her shoulder. 'Come down when you're ready. But don't worry about the yard – we can manage without you today.'

She held the tears in until he left. Then burying her head in her hands she cried.

Look for me and I'll be there.

She heard the echo of Spirit's voice so clearly it was almost as though he was really talking to her.

But you're not! she thought. *Oh, Spirit, you're not!* Her sobs wracked through her. She just wanted him back.

Ellie didn't come out of her bedroom until the afternoon. She felt almost as if all the crying had anaesthetized her. She walked on to the yard. Looking at the usual things going on – horses being groomed, ridden, the yards being swept – Ellie felt a wave of disbelief. It was almost impossible to her that everything could be going on as normal when Spirit was dead. The world should have stopped. She felt a sudden longing for Joe. Luke had been great but she wanted Joe there too, wanted his sympathy, his companionship.

Bracing herself, Ellie walked down to Spirit's stable. It was just as it had been when he had left it that morning. The fleece rug was thrown over his manger. Automatically, Ellie refolded it and made it look neat. Then she took his untouched haynet down.

Closing her eyes, she fought for control. The air of the stable seemed to smell of him. She breathed it in. She could almost imagine that she would open her eyes and see him standing there.

She stood there for a long moment before she opened her eyes and looked round the empty stable. Fighting back the tears that suddenly prickled again, she picked up the rug and left.

When the horsebox came driving down the lane later that afternoon, Luke told Ellie to go inside. 'I'll deal with Len.'

'No.' Ellie had a feeling that Luke was going to be in real trouble for digging the grave in the field. 'I'm not letting you face him on your own.'

'And I'm not letting you stay. You don't need to hear this conversation.' Luke steered her to the house. 'Please. Go inside. You're upset. You're not in a fit state for a row with Len. Go.'

Ellie hesitated, unused to letting herself be bossed around. But something deep down told her Luke was right. She was at the limits of her strength – she could not face her uncle right then. She looked into Luke's blue eyes and knew he'd be OK. 'Thanks.'

Luke smiled at her capitulation, one of his first smiles of the day. 'I'll come and find you when the worst is over.'

Ellie slipped up to her room. Sitting on her window seat, she watched as Len arrived back, saw his face as Luke told him the news – a brief nod as he told him about Spirit, a look of incredulity and anger as Luke told him about digging Spirit's grave.

Ellie could hear her uncle's bellow from all the way up in her bedroom. He let out a stream of swear words.

Luke stood unbothered as Len ranted and raged at him. He simply stood there with his arms folded, taking it.

Ellie didn't want to hear any more. She left the window seat and went to the bed. Lying down, she stared at the white painted ceiling. The pain came bowling back. Spirit was dead. However much Len raged about it, Spirit's body was now lying in the grave Luke had dug, the fresh soil dark and brown against the green of the grass. Her life would never be the same. Ellie turned on to her side and felt the sobs start all over again.

For the next few days, Ellie walked around in a

daze. Nothing really seemed to touch her. She did all the jobs she had to do, went to school and rode the horses, but all she wanted was just to get through each day, living for the moments when she could be alone and properly think about Spirit. Waking up each morning was awful. Ellie would blink her eyes open, feeling sick inside, as the realization of what had happened crashed over her. She would pull the covers over her head, unable to face the thought of another day without Spirit. But she had to. She couldn't stay in bed; she had to get up, carry on.

She spoke to Joe on the phone and told him what had happened. 'Oh, Els. I'm sorry,' he said in dismay.

Her heart clenched. The line was so clear it sounded as if he was just down the road. 'Yeah, well . . . How's everything with you?' She'd had emails from him, telling her he'd settled in well and saying how great Ray was.

'Good. But that's not important. How are you?'

She swallowed. She knew if he was too nice to her she'd cry. 'I'm . . .' she hesitated. What could she say? 'I'm doing OK,' she managed.

'How's Dad been?'

'Oh, you know. Mad with Luke for digging a grave for Spirit, shouting at everyone cos we're so busy. He hasn't found another groom to replace you yet.'

'And completely ignoring the fact Spirit's died?' Joe said, knowing his dad well.

'Yeah.' Her uncle had said very little to her about Spirit. She hadn't expected him to. After all, he hadn't offered her a single word of sympathy when her parents had died and so it didn't surprise her that he didn't try to comfort her in any way or make any exceptions to her workload on the yard. If anything he was making her work harder – now she had Joe's ponies to ride too.

'I'm so sorry,' Joe said again. 'I wish I was there.'

You could have been! It took an effort to bite the words back. It was hard not to feel angry. Since Spirit had died, anger was one of the feelings that most often swirled around inside her. Anger, bitterness, a feeling that it wasn't fair. 'I'd better go,' she said, suddenly not wanting to talk to him any more.

'Ring me again soon.'

'Yep,' Ellie said briefly. She clicked the phone off.

And after that, she didn't ring him again. She just couldn't face it. Every time she thought about him she wanted to blame him for not being there. If he rang her, she made excuses not to talk to him and she replied with just a few lines to his long emails, saying she was fine. It was what she said to anyone who asked. She felt disconnected from everyone and everything.

When she returned from school on the Monday,

eight days after Spirit's death, she found Len, Helen, Luke and Stuart gathered round Fern's stable door. John was inside. Just from the way they were all standing, Ellie could tell something was wrong.

'What's going on?' She went up to Luke.

His face looked serious. 'Grass sickness. It's Fern.'

Ellie stared at him uncomprehendingly. 'Grass sickness?' She knew it was a serious illness. 'But she was fine this morning.'

'It often comes on suddenly. She started looking colicky after you'd gone to school. She's got it bad. She's started with muscle tremors now. John will have to put her to sleep.'

Ellie waited for the shock to hit her, but it didn't. She felt immune, removed even from news as awful as that. 'Oh.' She saw Luke look at her in surprise.

'Oh?'

Ellie realized that her reaction wasn't what he'd been expecting. 'That's dreadful,' she faltered. 'What made it happen? Where did she catch it from? What about the others?'

'John said it's not contagious. It just happens in some horses. Their gut freezes – gets paralysed – and they can't digest any food. There are all sorts of factors that bring it on.'

'What about the foal?' The foal still didn't have a name. Len had been too busy to name her.

'She's up in the pony barn, upset at being separated from Fern. John's sedating her now before he puts Fern to sleep. She's been throwing herself at the door and trying to jump out of the stable.'

Compassion did start to flicker through Ellie at that. The chestnut filly must be so confused. Only a month ago, she'd been taken from her home and had to travel a long distance. Her mum had been the one security she had. Now she was separated from her too – this time forever. Ellie felt a rush of pain.

She swallowed. It was too much to deal with. She focused on becoming numb again. Numb was good.

John came down from the pony barn. 'OK, the foal's calm now. Let's see to the mare.'

'Bloody hell!' Len said, puffing out through his teeth. 'They're dropping like flies at the moment. She was a good mare too.' He glanced at Ellie and Luke. 'No digging a flamin' grave for this one.'

Ellie took a breath, trying to compose herself as he strode off. *I hate him*, she thought dully. Not letting herself think about what was happening in the stable, she walked slowly to the house, concentrating on the everyday things, getting changed, retying her hair in a ponytail. Why did so many bad things have to happen? She thought about her mum's saying: *every ending is another beginning*.

It was a stupid saying. The end of something wasn't always a beginning. There was no new beginning with Spirit's death; it was just the same old life only far greyer because it was without him, day after day when she felt as if a part of her was missing. And there would be no new beginning for the foal. Mum had been wrong. Sometimes ends were just ends.

Going back outside, she checked the whiteboard where Len wrote down who was to be ridden, then headed up to the pony barn. She had to ride Gem that afternoon. The blue roan pony had been quiet since Spirit died. All that week, whenever he had been in the field, he had lifted his head hopefully if he heard another horse being brought to the gate. Ellie was sure he had been looking for Spirit. She stroked his face as she reached his stall. 'You miss him too, don't you, boy?'

Gem nuzzled her. She thought how confused he must feel, his friend suddenly vanishing. Generally, most horses seemed to take loss in their stride, adapting, getting on with things without fretting. But Gem was a very sensitive horse. For a moment, it crossed her mind to try talking to him, to tell him. Maybe if he knew he'd stop looking for Spirit. She hesitated, her hand on Gem's neck. Should she?

But she would only be able to do it if she could

open herself up, clear her thoughts, fill herself with love and send it to Gem.

A lump formed in her throat. She couldn't do that now. She felt utterly drained. It was all she could do to keep herself going day after day, doing what she needed to, talking when spoken to. She couldn't, just couldn't, find the energy to give love too. And what would be the point? She hadn't been able to help Spirit when he had needed her most.

'I'm sorry,' she whispered to the pony. 'I just can't.'

Instead she groomed him, spending time stroking him and talking to him. Taking comfort from being with him, knowing that he missed Spirit too. To her relief, her uncle was still busy, organizing Fern's body being taken away, and so she rode on her own in the school. When she concentrated on riding, she could just about forget everything else. Not quite forget, but push things to the back of her mind at least.

She schooled Gem in circles, glad she was riding him and not feisty Milly or difficult Picasso. He was so easy and obliging, so keen to please; his only fault was his nervousness. Ellie focused on reassuring him and relaxing him. By the end of the session, he was going softly and well.

Afterwards, Ellie took him for a walk down the

lane to cool him off. As she rode along the drive, she let him stop at the bank of grass where she had taken Spirit to graze in the last few weeks of his life. The afternoon sun was warm and she dismounted, putting her arm over Gem's withers as he grazed. Looking down across the valley, she thought about all the times she had stood there with Spirit. She didn't want to remember too vividly in case it brought too much pain so she tiptoed around the memories. Shutting her eyes, she let herself remember in flashes – the curve of Spirit's face, the softness of his neck, the feel of his breath on her hands as he nuzzled her . . .

Suddenly she heard his voice as clearly as if he was standing beside her.

Look for me and I'll be there.

Her eyes shot open but there was just empty space, trees, grass, the driveway. Disappointment crashed over her – disappointment and exasperation at her own stupidity.

Spirit's dead, he isn't ever coming back, accept it, she told herself angrily. But as she remounted, the first lines of a poem that was read at her parents' funeral came back to her. It was about how when someone dies, they are not gone, not in the ground, buried and dead, but still there, around you in the air nearby.

It's just a poem, she thought. *When people –*

when horses – are dead, they're gone. They don't come back. You know they don't.

But Spirit's voice had sounded so real . . .

Despite herself, Ellie couldn't help glancing back to the bank as she rode away.

Chapter Ten

'Ellie?' Luke came to find Ellie as she mucked out Milly's stable. It was Saturday morning, almost two weeks since Spirit had died. 'Can you help me with Gabriel again today? He's been starting to throw his head around. Would you do your thing with him? Work out what the matter is?'

But Ellie was already shaking her head. She couldn't help. Helping would mean talking to Gabriel and, right now, she couldn't do that. She'd realized that with Gem the other day. 'Not today,' she mumbled. 'Another time.'

Luke frowned. Trying to ignore him, she continued to muck out. But it was hard – she could feel his eyes following her as she forked dirty straw into the wheelbarrow.

'Have you been to see the foal?' he said suddenly.

'No.'

'She's not looking great.'

Ellie knew the filly was refusing to drink the

replacement milk and the hard feed that Len had been trying to put her on. Ellie had overheard Stuart that morning say how the little foal wouldn't come anywhere near him, cramming herself into a corner of the stable and then flying at him with her teeth and hooves if he came close. Helen and Sasha had both tried too, but the foal had been the same with them. Since Fern had been put to sleep – disappearing as far as the foal was concerned – she had become even more distrustful of people. Ellie knew everyone was worried about her.

'She's dropping weight fast,' Luke went on. 'She's got to start drinking soon. There's talk of putting a tube in and feeding her that way, but that's going to freak her out even more. She'll hate people after that.'

Ellie didn't want to think about it; she turned back to her mucking out.

'Maybe you could have a try with her?'

Wishing he would just leave her alone, Ellie shut her eyes and shook her head, her heart aching.

She heard Luke turn and walk away without saying another word.

Ellie started to mechanically sweep the floor. She focused completely on the regular action, blocking out thoughts of the foal. She just couldn't cope. Other people could deal with it, not her.

Unbidden, a dream she'd had the night before

came into her mind. She'd had the same dream a few times now. She was always standing with Spirit, stroking him on a beach. Their minds were connected. Every time she dreamt it, he was urging her to talk to other horses.

Don't waste all you have learnt. You can do so much good. You can help.

I didn't help you.

You can help others.

Not without you, Spirit.

But I am with you. Just look.

Ellie rested on the broom. It had to be the guilt she was feeling at not helping the other horses that was giving her the dream. She should be helping; she knew she should. But how could she when she felt so empty?

After the mucking out was done, Ellie fetched Gem in from the field. It was an overcast day, the grey clouds pressing down towards the ground, and the air itself heavy with dampness.

Gem stood quietly as Ellie groomed him. Even without connecting with him, she could feel his depression. It matched her own, and after she had finished brushing him over she stood for a few moments, hugging him.

'Let's not go into the ménage today,' she said to him. 'Let's go out for a ride instead.' Her uncle was out at a show, with four of the livery horses and

Stuart, Helen and Sasha, leaving just Ellie and Luke on the yard.

Tacking Gem up, she mounted and headed towards the drive. Luke was coming out of the barn. 'I thought you were supposed to be schooling him?'

'I don't feel like it.'

Luke frowned. 'Where are you taking him?'

She shrugged. 'I don't know. Up to the mountains.' She just wanted to get away from the yard – be on her own.

Luke folded his arms. 'Is that a good idea? Why don't I come out with you? I'm supposed to be taking Gabriel out anyway.'

Ellie shook her head. 'I'll be fine.'

'Ellie!' Luke frowned. 'Let me come. Gem can still be really unreliable.'

Ellie didn't say anything. With a click of her tongue, she walked Gem on. But Luke stepped in front of her. The pony stopped in surprise, throwing his head up.

'Get out of my way,' she said, annoyed.

'No!' Luke argued. 'Stop being so stubborn. You're going to wait five minutes while I tack up.'

Ellie's emotions swirled. 'I don't have to do what you tell me!'

'You do. You're not thinking straight.'

'I am!' Tears welled in her eyes. 'I'm fine.'

'Really?' he snapped. 'There's a foal starving in one of the stables and you don't seem bothered. That's you being fine? I don't think so, Ellie.'

Ellie couldn't bear looking into his accusing eyes. He just didn't get it. No one did. No one knew how much she was hurting. 'Leave me alone!'

'No, I won't!' he responded. 'I'm not going to let you pretend this isn't happening. The foal is refusing to eat. You could at least try to get her to drink. You're amazing with horses who have problems – horses who are sick.'

'I wasn't amazing with Spirit!' The words wrenched out of her. 'I couldn't get *him* to eat!'

'Ellie! This isn't about Spirit!' Luke exclaimed. 'No one could have done anything for him. Not you. Not anyone. Even if you could have got him to eat it wouldn't have changed anything anyway. The foal's different. If she started to feed she'd be healthy again.' He stared at her. 'I can't believe you're just opting out like this.'

'Believe it,' Ellie muttered numbly.

Luke swore. 'For heaven's sake, Ellie! Will you stop being so wrapped up in yourself? Spirit's dead. Deal with it!'

Anger burst through her. 'Don't you dare tell me to deal with it!' she shouted back. 'You have no idea what it's like for me!' Her eyes blazed. 'I've lost Mum, Dad, Spirit, Joe. You haven't got a clue. God,

Luke! You say I'm wrapped up in myself? *Me?* You're the selfish one! You have no idea how much you hurt people. No idea at all!' She saw the shock on his face, the start of a look of contrition.

'Ellie, I –' He reached for the reins again.

'*No!*' She kicked Gem hard. The startled pony leapt forward, almost knocking Luke down. Ellie pulled his head round and set off at a canter. The pony's hooves slid and clattered on the concrete but Ellie didn't care. She galloped him out of the yard and turned into the woods. Unnerved by her rage, Gem raced up the path. Ellie ducked as branches swept at her face but still she pushed on, not caring about exposed roots or ruts in the track, just wanting to put as much distance between her and Luke as she could. She wanted to gallop and gallop and never stop.

Gem emerged from the trees on to the mountainside. It had started to rain now and the wind was blustery on the exposed slopes, but Ellie barely felt the drops hitting her face. She kicked her heels into Gem's sides. He stretched his head and neck out, galloping now into the rain. Ellie lost herself in the drumming of his hooves. Why did Spirit have to die? Why had he been taken away too?

Look for me and I'll be there. His words echoed.

'But you're not!' she sobbed furiously. 'You're not, Spirit! You're not!'

Gem was starting to tire. She could feel his strides getting more laboured as the mountain got steeper and the ground rougher under his hooves, grass giving way to scree and bare patches of mud. Ellie could barely see ahead of her now the mist had descended.

As she saw Gem's ears start to flick uncertainly and felt him slow further, she wondered if she should stop. But that would mean turning round, facing everything that was waiting back at the yard. No. She pushed him on.

A sheep emerged from the mist. Gem shied violently. Ellie was thrown to one side and had to grab his neck and mane to try and stay on. She struggled to get back into the saddle, having lost her stirrups, but her struggles upset him even more and he swung round in alarm. She felt herself slipping down the side of him. 'Whoa, Gem!' she gasped.

But Gem, never the quietest pony, was caught in a panic at feeling her grab his mane and saddle. He reared, sending her thumping to the ground. She saw the reins fly past her, tried to grab them, but it was too late – Gem plunged forward and raced away back down the mountainside, heading for the safety of the stables.

For a moment, Ellie lay on the hard ground, dazed and shocked. She sat up, automatically checking for injuries. Her back and arm hurt but she hadn't broken anything. She looked around her. The rain was soaking into her thin T-shirt. Suddenly she was aware how cold and wet she was.

Collecting her thoughts, she struggled to her feet. She had no idea whereabouts on the mountain she was and she began to head down through the mist, rubbing her bare arms. Where was Gem? She hoped he would get home all right. Now her anger had faded, she began to see how stupid she'd been. She hadn't even thought about the rough ground. Gem could have tripped, fallen, caught his foot in a rabbit hole. Tears welled up inside her as she looked through the mist. There was absolutely no one there; she was completely on her own, freezing cold, soaked, miserable – and worried about Gem.

Just get home, she thought. *Get back to the stables. See he's OK.*

But after Ellie had been walking ten minutes, she wondered if she was going in the right direction. She'd thought she would be in the woods by now but she was still walking on the mountain slopes. The only sounds were the baaing of sheep through the mist and she couldn't see more than a metre in front of her. There was no track to follow, no walls or footpaths, only her own sense of the way she had come.

Anxiety flickered through her. If she got lost, it

could be really dangerous. No one would find her in the mist and her clothes gave no protection against the weather. She walked on further but still couldn't see the woods. Her legs ached and she was shivering now. She knew she should continue walking to keep warm, but all she wanted to do was stop and cry.

She felt as if she had reached the very end of her strength; she was exhausted. Seeing a grey rock, she sat down on it and buried her head in her hands. *I can't do this any more*, she thought helplessly. *I just can't go on.*

Tears seeped through her fingers, hot against her damp, cold skin and she started to sob.

She didn't know how long she had been crying, but suddenly through her despair she felt the air around her change. There was the sound of a hoof hitting a stone. She froze and then glanced up. Was it Gem? No, deep down she knew with an absolute certainty that it wasn't. She knew that feeling in the air but it couldn't be . . .

A whinny rang out.

Ellie felt as if every cell in her body had just been given an electric shock. She would know that whinny anywhere. She couldn't breathe. Even her heart seemed to have stopped beating.

A grey horse appeared through the mist. Stopping beside her, he gently nuzzled her hands.

Chapter Eleven

'Spirit?'

The word choked out of Ellie. Suddenly she couldn't feel the rain or cold any more. Her whole being was focused on the horse's warm breath whispering across her fingers, the sight of his dark eyes, his forelock falling across his face. 'How . . .' Ellie's voice faltered as she stared at him. *How?*

I have come back.

But . . .

You can *go* on. *I am here.*

So many questions whirled through Ellie's brain and for a moment she was reminded of another time – when Spirit had first spoken to her. Like this, it had seemed impossible, but, just as she had then, she gave in to the impossible. Whether it was a dream or hallucination, whether it was real or not, at that moment she didn't care. She just wanted so much for it to be true.

Reaching up, she touched his warm neck. The

next second she was on her feet hugging him, burying her head in his mane, shaking and sobbing, but this time with happiness and relief. Her grief rolled away. Spirit was here now, with her.

I've missed you so much. Oh, Spirit. I couldn't bear it.

You have to. You have to carry on.

But I can't live without you.

Then I will be here. I will stay.

Like this?

Yes, for as long as you need me.

You're a ghost?

I am Spirit.

Ellie looked at him wonderingly, realizing she didn't care if he was a ghost or not; the important thing was that he'd come back to her, that they could talk again.

You must *keep going,* he told her. *Help other horses.*

Ellie thought about the foal and guilt washed over her.

Spirit read her thoughts. *She has a part to play in your life. Go to her and help her – for her sake, for your own.*

Ellie didn't know what he meant but she knew she must do as he said. But as she looked round, she remembered the reality of her situation. *I don't know how to get home.*

I will show you.

Spirit began to lead her down the mountain, his hooves finding a safe pathway, his eyes seeing through the mist.

When they reached the woods, she was able to see him more clearly. He looked healthy again. Even the old scars on his legs and shoulders had healed. His eyes were glowing and he seemed young and strong. She couldn't stop looking at him. Their gazes met and she felt the numbness that had been wrapped around her heart, since the day he died, melt. As they reached the edge of the wood, Spirit stopped.

Go on without me now. But do not worry. I will be near you. Always now.

Ellie's fingers clenched for a moment on his mane. *Have faith.*

She released her grip and watched him fade away. But shutting her eyes, she could still feel his presence, feel his energy swirling around her. He *was* there. Taking a deep breath, she walked out of the woods.

The rain had stopped, and as she walked up the driveway, she heard a yell. Luke had spotted her from the stable yard. He came running to meet her. His face was pale, his eyes shot through with worry, and all trace of his usual amused expression had vanished from his face.

'Ellie! Christ! I was so worried! Gem came back half an hour ago on his own. I went out looking in the woods but couldn't find you. I've been worried sick.'

He reached her and grabbed her in his arms. She felt herself pulled against his chest. 'I'm OK,' she said dazedly.

'You're soaked through!' Luke looked at her wet clothes. 'Where the hell have you been?'

'On the mountainside. Is Gem all right?'

'Yeah, a few scratches and his reins are broken but otherwise he's fine. What were you doing on the mountainside?'

'I went up there and fell off. I tried to find my way down, but it was misty and I got lost.'

Luke hugged her again. All Ellie could think about was Spirit. He was back. She remembered the promise she'd made to him and pulled out of Luke's arms. 'The foal. I want to go and see her.' She started hurrying past him.

'The foal?' Luke caught up with her in a few strides. 'You can't go and see her now. You've just been lost in the rain, you need to get changed, sit down –'

'I'll get changed, but I won't sit down. I'm going to see her.'

Luke shook his head incredulously, but put his hands up in surrender. 'All right, all right. I give up with you. Whatever. Just get some dry clothes on first.'

Five minutes later, Ellie was changed and back on the yard. Luke had dried Gem off and he was out in the field, no worse for his adventure. Luke watched her as she went to the filly's stable.

'Leave me alone with her,' she told him.

He nodded, still looking anxious. She had the feeling he thought she was on the edge of going slightly mad, but Ellie had never felt more sane in her life. All her numbness and weariness had vanished. She didn't know if she could help the foal but she was going to try.

The foal stood in a corner of the stable. Her head was low, her ribs protruding, her chestnut coat looked coarse and her eyes were dull. For a moment, Ellie was painfully reminded of Spirit when he had been ill. The foal was so young that even a few days without anything to eat had left her looking half starved. But Ellie sensed something beyond the foal being physically weak, something that she had never felt with Spirit – a sense that the foal had given up.

Ellie felt her heart going out to the little filly. She knew that feeling. She had been engulfed by it for the past two weeks. But Spirit had come to her in her hour of need, and thinking about him sent determination flooding through her. If there was any way she could help the foal, she would.

She walked over. Despite her weakness, the foal moved warily backwards. 'It's OK,' Ellie soothed, holding her hand out. The filly moved further into the corner, staring at her with deep distrust.

Ellie remembered what Spirit had taught her – sometimes you just had to wait with horses. You could never force them to talk, just be there, open yourself and wait. She stepped back and sat down on some clean straw near the manger.

The minutes ticked past. Gradually the foal began to relax. Ellie shut her eyes and focused on her breathing, clearing her mind of everything but the foal.

It's OK, she thought. *I'm not going to hurt you. You can talk to me.*

Keeping her eyes shut, she focused on where the foal was, felt her energy, weak and fading. Compassion welled up inside her and gathering up all her own energy she let it flow to the foal.

I'm listening. If you want to, we can talk.

She didn't know how long she sat there, but slowly she felt the familiar sensation of their minds merging. The foal's thoughts were clear – as clear as Spirit's were to her. An image of a chestnut mare came into her mind. It was Fern. Ellie could feel the foal's aching sense of loss and confusion. *Where has she gone?*

She's died, Ellie thought back.

Died? The filly didn't seem to understand.

Gone.

Forever?

Yes, forever. Ellie sent all the love she could to the little filly. She had been through so much, moving from her first home when she was so young and then having her mother taken away. Standing up, Ellie went over. The filly stayed where she was this time. Ellie touched her neck. 'There now,' she murmured.

The filly trembled. She felt so fragile; her bones sticking out under her tightly stretched skin. Ellie began to move her hands around her body, starting at her neck and working her way very gently over her just as she used to do with Spirit.

She could feel the foal's intense loss as if it was her own. It was a loss that hurt like a physical pain, a pain that overwhelmed any desire to eat or drink.

Ellie's heart went out to the filly. She was just a baby. *You don't have to carry this*, she told her gently. *Let me take your pain.*

Very gradually, she felt the foal's energy readjust and her breathing began to slow. Her eyelids fluttered and her head dropped down. Ellie moved to her face, touching her forehead. The foal's legs trembled. With a sigh, she let the worst of the grief go and sank down into the straw. Ellie knelt beside her and stroked her head.

There, you're safe now. She felt an absolute desire to love and protect the foal. To look after her.

She didn't know how long she sat there, but eventually she felt the connection between their minds close as the exhausted foal finally fell asleep, her muzzle resting on Ellie's knees. Ellie gently kissed her forehead. The tingling in her fingers faded. She blinked. It felt as if they had been lost in another world for a while. Now, she looked round at the stable, seeing the details – the strands of straw in the bed, the dust in the shafts of light, the black water bucket.

There was a noise at the door. Ellie turned. It was Luke. 'How's it going?' He saw the foal lying with her. 'You've got close to her anyway.'

Ellie nodded.

'Do you need anything?' he asked.

'Could you bring me some fresh milk and feed for her?'

Luke returned five minutes later with a bucket of milk that was made for orphaned foals and some foal mix in a bucket. The sound of the door opening woke the foal. Her head lifted and she looked round, her eyes slightly dazed. Ellie immediately soothed her. 'It's OK.'

'Shall I stay?' Luke said.

Ellie shook her head. 'No.' She wanted to be alone with the foal for longer. She needed to get her to drink.

He left and Ellie offered the milk to the foal. Putting her fingers into it, she held them up. The foal sniffed her fingers and licked some milk off them. Ellie offered her some more, each time lowering her hand until it was in the warm milk for longer. The foal sought for her fingers, her muzzle going into the milk too, and then to Ellie's delight she started to suck up the milk herself. Ellie stroked her neck and listened to the rhythmical noises as the foal drained the bucket. She licked the remaining milk from the bottom and then gave a long, contented sigh.

Ellie could feel the change in her now. It was as though the pall of sadness that had been lying over her had lifted. She started to feed her from the other bucket, and soon the foal was nuzzling up the grain from Ellie's hands.

Outside, Ellie could hear the bustling sounds of the yard, but inside the stable it was peaceful. She wanted to look after the foal, and help her get used to life without her mother.

'I'll be here for you,' she vowed. 'Your mum might

not be, but I'll do everything I can.' She stroked her again and, as she did so, felt a warm breath on her shoulder. She froze.

Spirit?

Yes, I am here.

Ellie looked round, but the stable was empty.

Shut your eyes and you will see me.

Closing her eyes, Ellie reached out for him, and suddenly she *could* see him standing there beside her. She reached up and he touched her hand with his muzzle. She felt the softness of the skin, felt his lips rub across her palm, and then he breathed on her hair.

Ellie felt a rush of joy. He was back again. He really was there.

You've helped her. She felt his contentment.

I don't know what I did. I just talked to her and touched her. She seemed to like it.

You have healing hands.

Ellie swallowed. *They didn't heal you.*

Nothing could have helped me, but you can help others.

For a moment, Ellie was too overwhelmed to say anything.

Use your gifts well.

I will, she promised.

A picture came into her mind and she saw the filly in the field with Gem.

You think I should turn them out together? she asked him.

Yes. They will be good for each other. They both need you, but they need each other too.

Ellie realized he was right. The foal needed the company of another horse now her mother was gone and Gem was missing Spirit. He adored the filly and he was so gentle he would never hurt her.

When she wakes up, feed her again and then turn them out.

Ellie nodded.

For a while, neither of them said any more. The foal had fallen asleep again, seemingly oblivious to Spirit. Ellie simply sat with the foal's head resting on her knees, Spirit's presence beside her. A feeling of contentment sank over her, taking away any desire to do anything. She wanted to freeze time, hold the moment forever. After all the grief and all the bleakness, she was happy again. Spirit had come back to her and this time he would never go away.

She sighed and finally fell asleep herself. Standing quietly beside her, the grey ghost watched over her and the little foal.

'Ellie?'

At the sound of Luke's voice, Ellie blinked her

eyes open and sat up, wondering where she was. She realized she was in the stable; the filly was stirring beside her, Luke was at the door . . .

She glanced around quickly. Spirit had left. But he would come back. She knew that with a certainty that ran through every bone in her body.

Luke came into the stable. 'Are you OK? You've been in here ages. It's almost feedtime.'

'I . . . I fell asleep.'

Luke crouched down. 'I guess you needed it. You got the foal to drink then?'

The filly nuzzled Ellie. Her eyes were brighter now, refreshed. Putting her head into the bucket, she licked the bottom and then nudged Ellie hard.

'I think she wants some more,' Ellie smiled.

'I'll get it,' Luke offered.

As he left the stable, Ellie stood up. She busied herself with the foal, patting and stroking her, dusting the straw off her. Even without being connected to her, Ellie could feel the new lightness around the filly.

Luke returned. Ellie took the bucket from him. 'Here you are.' This time, the foal didn't need any encouragement; she plunged her head in. Ellie and Luke watched her drink, her fluffy tail swishing from side to side.

'You know, we can't keep calling her "the foal",' Ellie said.

'No, we need a name for her,' Luke agreed. 'You'd better think of something.'

Ellie glanced at him. It was hard to believe it was only that morning she had shouted at him and galloped off on Gem. She thought of the things she had said to him. Guilt flashed through her as she remembered how he had been there for her in the last few weeks. How he had always been the one who cared enough to tell her what she didn't want to hear. How he had been there to pick up the pieces and help her through. She hadn't been fair.

'I'm sorry about earlier,' she said.

Luke shot her a sideways look. 'For galloping off or for yelling at me?'

'Both.'

He smiled wryly. 'Guess I asked for it.'

But Ellie didn't want to be let off the hook. 'You didn't. You were just trying to make me listen. I *am* sorry. You're not selfish. I shouldn't have said that.'

He looked at her. Part of her suddenly wanted to shut up, say nothing more, but she also wanted to him to know how grateful she was. He deserved that. 'Thank you,' she went on doggedly. 'I mean it. Thank you for everything you've done. For being there when Spirit died. For digging the grave. For sorting stuff out afterwards. For telling me it was time when it was.'

Luke regarded her for a moment and then smiled. ''S OK.' He put his arm over her shoulders and turned back to watch the foal.

Ellie could feel the weight of his arm, the warmth of his body next to hers. It felt strange being so close to him in such a relaxed way. She was used to hugging Joe like this but not Luke. She wondered what Joe would say when he heard about the day. For the first time in a week, she found herself wanting to speak to him, to tell him about things.

'So, what did you do?' Luke asked, looking at the foal. 'How did you get her to drink?'

'I just talked to her.'

Luke gave a short laugh. 'I should've known! Horse-whisperer!' He pulled her in tighter and for a second all she could think about was the feeling of his arm around her shoulders. She tried to focus on the foal.

'I think she should be turned out with Gem. He's missing Spirit and she needs company,' Ellie said, her voice slightly breathless.

Luke frowned. 'With Gem? Put a gelding and a foal together?'

'It'll be fine,' Ellie promised, trusting Spirit's advice completely. 'I know it will.'

Luke looked down at her. 'You're incredible. Do you know that?' Ellie felt her cheeks warming as his gaze swept intently over her face. 'Maddening – yes. Infuriating – yes. But you're like no one I've ever met before.'

Staring up at him, all Ellie could think about was his eyes, his face, the way he was looking at her. *This is LUKE!* a voice screamed in her head.

With a supreme effort, she forced herself to step back. His arm dropped from her shoulders, his face assuming its usual amused expression.

'I . . . I think I'll fetch Gem and turn them out,' Ellie stammered.

Luke raised his eyebrows. 'You'd better see if he's forgiven you for that gallop up the mountain yet. Poor Gem!'

Ellie walked to the door, not sure what had just happened. Reaching the door, she looked back. Luke was stroking the foal.

A name came into Ellie's head as she looked at them. 'Hope,' she said. 'That's what we should call her.'

Luke nodded. 'I like it.' He turned to the foal. 'What do you think? Do you want to be called Hope?'

The foal snorted.

Luke's mouth quirked into a smile. 'Well, I'd say that was yes. There's obviously nothing to this horse-whispering business. Maybe I should try it more often!'

'Maybe you should,' Ellie grinned back and, with her heart lighter than it had been for a while, she left the stable and went up the yard.

Sunset . . .

The sun sank down behind the mountains. Ellie stood at the field gate, watching Gem and Hope. It was still early days, after all it was unusual for a foal and gelding to be field companions, but from the moment they'd been put out together, Gem had been like a nanny, nuzzling the little foal, watching over her protectively. Ellie watched him graze, his eyes never leaving his young charge. For the first time since Spirit had died, she felt a new happiness in him.

To her surprise, when her uncle rang to see how the foal was doing and Luke had suggested Hope as a name, her uncle had agreed. Soon after, Ellie had rung Joe to tell him that the foal had started to drink.

'That's brilliant! And how are you?' She could hear the anxiety in his voice.

'I'm OK,' she replied.

'Really? You haven't said much in your mails and I'd kind of got the feeling you were avoiding me.'

'It's been a difficult week. But I *am* feeling OK now. I'm sorry about not talking to you much.'

'That's all right. I've just been worried about you.'

Ellie felt the last remnants of her anger with him slip away. He might have gone, but he did care about her, she knew he did. They were still best friends. 'What's happening in Canada then?' she asked.

'All sorts. We're visiting a massage clinic tomorrow. Yesterday was great too – we were doing all this work using ground poles with unbroken horses.'

Joe had told her all about it. Remembering it now, Ellie smiled as she leant against the gate.

Every ending is a new beginning, she thought, remembering her mum's saying. She shouldn't have doubted it. Spirit's death *had* been a new beginning for her – the start of her life without him in the flesh but still very much with her, just in a new and different way. And new beginnings had come from Fern's death too. A bond had formed that day between Ellie and the filly. Ellie remembered the first time she had seen the foal and the connection she'd felt between them. Maybe the bond had always been there, but it was only today that she had allowed it to start to blossom. Where would it lead? She didn't know. She looked in the direction of the field where Spirit's body was buried and thought of his words on the mountainside about the filly: *she has a part to play in your life.* What had he meant?

There was a soft snort behind her. *There is so much more to come.*

Spirit! Almost not daring to look, she reached out with her hand and felt her fingers touch his mane. Turning slowly, she saw him standing there. All thoughts of the future and what would happen with the foal faded from her mind. All that mattered was now.

Oh, Spirit. I am so glad you're here. She touched his face wonderingly and he gazed back at her. *I'm so glad you came back to me today.*

Spirit rested his muzzle on her shoulder. They were together again, where they belonged. Not even death could part them.

They stood together, girl and horse, surrounded by their love, as the rays of the setting sun streaked golden and pink across the midsummer sky.

Turn over to enjoy an extract from
another enchanting book about Ellie
and her beloved horse, Spirit.

Ellie Carrington leant against the gate of the circular menage, a horse-training manual open in her hands, the breeze blowing through her long, wavy blonde hair. In the ring, a chestnut pony cantered round her cousin, Joe.

'He needs to go slower, I think!' Ellie called. 'It says here: "the horse should settle into a steady trot". Can you slow Solo down while keeping him going round the outside?'

'I think so.' Joe moved so he was level with the pony's neck. Solo instantly bounced to a stop. With a snort, he turned and raced in the other direction at an even faster canter than before.

Ellie giggled. 'Think again!'

Joe frowned in concentration, his greeny-grey eyes intent, his sandy-brown hair flopping over his forehead. His father's horse-showing yard – High Peak Stables – had a top-class reputation and Joe had ridden in the show ring all his life, but Ellie knew he was happiest like this, at home, working with a young horse. That morning, he was trying out a training technique called 'join-up'. It was a method based on understanding how horses acted in the wild, and using body language to communicate with them. It was particularly good for young horses and ponies like Solo when they were first being trained to wear a saddle and carry a rider.

Joe moved towards the pony's hindquarters, but

that only made Solo go faster. He tried stepping closer to Solo's head, which made the pony stop, whizz round and change direction again. Joe stayed calm and patient, though. Finally, while staying level with the pony's stomach, he tried stepping back. It worked. Solo slowed to a trot.

Solo trotted round the ring several times, his movement gradually becoming rhythmical and relaxed. Whenever he slowed down too much, Joe moved towards his hindquarters, sending him on. After a few minutes, he began to experiment with making Solo change direction, using just eye contact and the positioning of his body. It was very peaceful in the early morning. The only sounds were the thud of Solo's hooves on the sand and his occasional snort ringing through the air. Behind the schooling ring rose the mountains of north Derbyshire, their peaks and ridges silhouetted against the pale blue sky. Sheep dotted the slopes, the black-faced ewes grazing, the lambs bouncing around.

'What should I look for next?' Joe called.

Ellie checked the book again. 'His ear should tilt towards you and he should start to lick and maybe chew. His head might lower even more.'

As she spoke, Solo's muzzle reached to the ground and he did exactly as she had just said. 'There! Look! That's him saying to you that he wants to join-up.'

Turning away from Solo, Joe dropped his gaze to

the floor, lowering his head and rounding his shoulders. Solo slowed to a walk and then halted, looking at Joe's new non-threatening body position. Ellie had read that this was the crucial moment, the time when the pony would make the choice whether to come in and be close to the human in the middle, or decide to stay away. If he chose to come in, it would be his way of saying he trusted Joe and they could start backing him. If he chose to stay away, then Joe would turn back and continue to drive him on.

Solo hesitated and then walked towards the centre, stopping beside Joe's shoulder. *Yes!* Ellie thought, her breath leaving her in a rush. It had happened just like the book said it should!

Joe looked outwardly calm, but Ellie was sure he was just as delighted as she was – he didn't need the book to know what Solo coming in meant. After turning to gently rub the pony's face between his eyes, he walked away and Solo followed him. Wherever Joe went, so did the pony. He didn't *have* to be with the boy; he was choosing to be. By responding to the signals Solo had sent – the pony's way of saying in horse language that he wanted to be friends – Joe had shown Solo that he understood him. The first building blocks of trust had been laid.

'It's worked!' Joe said, coming to the gate.

He and Ellie smiled at each other, sharing the moment.

'Are you going to try putting the saddle on now?' Ellie asked.

Joe nodded.

Ellie had seen ponies being backed quite a few times and knew that usually they would buck and fight, scared of the weight of the saddle and the tightening of the girth round their stomachs. But as Joe put a headcollar on Solo, then took the saddle from the fence to place it on Solo's back, the pony stood quietly. As Joe fastened the girth, Solo tensed, but Joe reassured him, talking gently, and the pony relaxed again, trusting what Joe was doing.

When Joe asked him to walk on, the pony walked calmly beside him as if he'd had a saddle on his back every day of his life.

It was incredible to watch. Ellie remembered the last time she'd seen a pony being backed. It had been in New Zealand, before her parents had died. She'd been with her dad. They'd watched as the pony had thrown itself around.

'There has to be a better way,' her dad had said to her then.

Dad would have loved to see this, Ellie thought wistfully. *Mum too.*

Loss welled up painfully inside her. Last July, both her parents had died in a car crash. She could barely remember the time straight after, her grief had been completely overwhelming. But over the eight months since then, the intense pain had gradually faded. She still missed them every day, but most of the time now she could get by OK. Or at least she could until something like this happened – a moment that she would want to share with them – and then the fact that they were gone, that she would never see them again, would hit her full-on.

She had many tricks for dealing with the pain. Now, she focused on holding her breath, counting to ten and back again, waiting for the feelings to subside. She hoped Joe was too busy with Solo to notice. He would only ask what was wrong if he saw she was upset and she didn't like to talk about her mum and dad with anyone apart from Spirit.

As Ellie pictured Spirit's pricked ears and dark wise eyes, she felt as if the pain inside her was being wrapped in a blanket. Just the thought of Spirit could comfort her. It felt like he had been in her life forever, but it had only been two months since she had first seen him at a horse sale, bought him and led him back here to High Peak Stables. Back then the countryside had been gripped by winter, snow hugging the bare peaks, a bitter wind blowing across the yard every day, but now the air was warmer and yellow daffodils danced around the fence posts.

Ellie looked around. Even with spring softening the rugged bleakness of the mountains, the countryside here in the Peak District was far from the lush rolling hills of New Zealand where she had grown up. It still felt like a landscape that she didn't quite belong in – part of a life that wasn't really hers.

She had wanted to stay with her gran in New Zealand, but it had eventually been decided it was best for Ellie to move to England to live with her Uncle Len and sixteen-year-old cousin, Joe. Being only fourteen, she had no say in the matter. She wondered what her life would be like if she'd hadn't left New Zealand. It was hard to know how to feel about that, because then, of course, she wouldn't have met Joe or bought Spirit. Her mum had used to have a saying: 'every ending is another beginning'. It was true, she realized. So many new things had begun since her life in New Zealand had ended . . .